WITHDRAWN

Goddess Girls

CALLIOPE
THE
MUSE

Goddess Girls

CALLIOPE
THE
MUSE

JOAN HOLUB & SUZANNE WILLIAMS

Aladdin

NEW YORK   LONDON   TORONTO   SYDNEY   NEW DELHI

ALADDIN

An imprint of Simon & Schuster Children's Publishing Division

1230 Avenue of the Americas, New York, New York 10020

First Aladdin hardcover edition August 2016

Text copyright © 2016 by Joan Holub and Suzanne Williams

Jacket illustration copyright © 2016 by Glen Hanson

Also available in an Aladdin paperback edition.

All rights reserved, including the right of reproduction in whole or in part in any form.

ALADDIN is a trademark of Simon & Schuster, Inc., and related logo is

a registered trademark of Simon & Schuster, Inc.

For information about special discounts for bulk purchases,

please contact Simon & Schuster Special Sales at

1-866-506-1949 or business@simonandschuster.com.

The Simon & Schuster Speakers Bureau can bring authors to your live event.

For more information or to book an event, contact the Simon & Schuster Speakers Bureau at

1-866-248-3049 or visit our website at www.simonspeakers.com.

Designed by Karin Paprocki

The text of this book was set in Baskerville.

Manufactured in the United States of America 0716 FFG

2 4 6 8 10 9 7 5 3 1

Library of Congress Control Number 2016937781

ISBN 978-1-4814-5005-8 (hc)

ISBN 978-1-4814-5004-1 (pbk)

ISBN 978-1-4814-5006-5 (eBook)

CONTENTS

To our mega-marvelous readers!
Martha H., Olivia C., Ela N., Zubin N., Megan D., Keny Y.,
Koko Y., Connie S., Latoya H., Keira J., Shelby Lynn J. &
Virginia Anna J., Madison W., Dawn H., Kristina S.,
McKay O. & Reese O., Ariel P., Patrona C., Tiffany & Justin W.,
Madison S., Madison S., Paris O., Christine D-H., Khanya S.,
Lillia L., Ryanna L., Amanda W., Caitlin and Hannah R.,
Ariana F., The Andrade Family and Alba C., Ana B.,
Jasmine R., Sophie R., Alyssa B., Ally M., Keyra M., Lana W.,
Vivian Z., Grace P., Jessica S., and you!
—J. H. & S. W.

Prologue

U P IN THE SKY THE CHARIOT DRIVEN BY HELIOS the sun god had begun its daily descent toward the west. School was over for the day at Mount Olympus Academy, so most students were in the cafeteria eating dinner.

After glancing around to make sure the coast was clear, a two-legged figure in a hooded black cloak hurried across the marble-tiled outdoor courtyard.

Holding an empty bag, this sneak slipped in through the Academy's bronze front doors, then padded softly past the entryway and turned down an empty hall, searching for a particular classroom.

Squeak! Suddenly a door swung open. A tall, one-eyed giant lumbered out into the hallway. It was Mr. Cyclops, an MOA teacher. The cloaked figure gasped and darted through the nearest door to hide. The room turned out to be some kind of storage closet, with reams of papyrus, feather pens, and textscrolls.

Heart thumping, the intruder crouched on hands and knees under the closet's bottom shelf and waited until the teacher had passed. *Phew! That was close.* The figure crept out into the hall again. In a flash it scurried over to the classroom Mr. Cyclops had just vacated. Luckily, the door had been left slightly ajar. The hooded figure pushed through it and went straight to a large, long table in the middle of the room.

At last! Quickly now!

The figure's eyes roved over the table, which was entirely covered by a three-dimensional map, one that was extraordinarily realistic, with roads, valleys, villages, castles with moats, and mountains that looked to be a foot tall. Strange, miniature-size scaly beasts dove and splashed in the magical map's oceans. As amazing as the beasts were, however, they weren't what the figure had come for. Its eyes glittered at the sight of dozens of little hero statues scattered around the map, which was actually a game board.

The three-inch high statues were game pieces. Each one represented a real mortal hero. Students in Mr. Cyclops's Hero-ology classes moved them around the map during certain class assignments. And whatever

3

happened to the little hero game pieces on this map would also magically happen to the corresponding living, breathing real-life heroes down on Earth.

After plucking all the hero statues from the game board, the thieving figure stashed them in the bag it had brought, then left the room.

Retracing its steps, this sneak quickly made its way out of the Academy unseen. Once outside, it hurried down the building's granite steps and back across the marble courtyard.

After reaching the far side of the courtyard, the figure entered a grove of olive trees. It took a trail from there, descending from Mount Olympus to Earth.

Mission accomplished!

1

Architecture-ology Blues

One and a half weeks later . . .

TWELVE-YEAR-OLD CALLIOPE HAD JUST TAKEN her seat in her last-period Architecture-ology class on Friday afternoon when she heard a sound.

"Psst!"

She glanced over at Medusa, the green-skinned, snaky-haired mortal girl whose desk was next to hers. Was Medusa trying to get her attention? Or had her snakes simply been hissing?

This puzzle was solved when Medusa leaned her way. "I heard you gave that author guy, Homer lots of inspiration, while he was writing *The Iliad* and *The Odyssey*. True?"

Calliope's long wavy red hair, which was gathered in a loose ponytail at the back of her neck, bounced a bit as she nodded. "True." Inspiring those two scroll-books had made her kind of famous. Though not as famous as they'd made the fifteen-year-old author Homer himself!

"Then maybe you could help me too?" Medusa asked. "I've got a paper due on Monday for Revenge-ology class, and I'm totally blanking. Can't come up with any ideas for it. None that are good, anyway."

"What's the topic?" Calliope asked matter-of-factly.

She'd only begun to attend Mount Olympus Academy a month or so ago, but already she'd gotten used to fellow students asking her for ideas on this and that.

Most of them had heard the story of how she had inspired Homer. While writing about a mortal hero named Odysseus, Homer had pleaded eloquently for her helpful ideas, asking her to "sing" to him of Odysseus, "the man of twists and turns."

Just thinking about Homer made Calliope sigh dreamily. He had such a great vocabulary and was so incredibly talented. And she adored his cute spiky blue hair. But, unfortunately, she could only crush on him from afar. Because except for when she'd been helping him with his books, he seemed totally blind to the fact that she was even alive!

Medusa leaned toward Calliope again. "Well?" Emphasizing her request, the snakes on top of her head curved themselves into a dozen scaly, green question marks.

Calliope snapped to attention. She'd been so lost in her thoughts about Homer that she'd missed Medusa's reply to her question! "Sorry. Spaced out for a minute. What did you just say?"

Medusa let out a frustrated little huff and glanced up to be sure Mr. Libon, the teacher, wasn't yet looking for everyone's attention, ready to start class. "I *said* that Ms. Nemesis told us our papers could be about anything related to revenge."

"Hmm. Pretty wide open, then." Calliope tapped her chin with an index finger, thinking. "This is just off the top of my head," she said after a moment, "but maybe you could write about the relationship between revenge and war. How wars are often started as an act of revenge. Like the Trojan War. It began because

King Menelaus wanted revenge against Paris after Paris stole his wife, Helen."

"Maybe," Medusa said with a shrug. If her snakes had had shoulders, they probably would have shrugged too. "Got any other ideas?" she asked.

Calliope didn't mind that her first idea didn't appeal to Medusa much. Sometimes it took a few tries to hit on the very thing that would catch someone's interest and generate true inspiration! Her brown eyes lit up as a new idea came to her.

"Or you could write about the *psychology* of revenge," she told Medusa. "Like, what causes vengeful feelings, the purpose those feelings serve, and if we should resist those feelings or give in to them. That kind of thing— Oh, wait," she said, interrupting herself. "Here's another idea! You could interview MOA students about times when they've taken revenge on someone and—"

"Good afternoon, class," interrupted their Architecture-ology teacher, Mr. Libon. He'd stood up from his desk at the front of the room, wearing his usual sandals, which each had a single tassel for decoration. Though he was medium height, he looked plumper than he really was because he wore a tunic with dozens of pockets, each filled with drawing tools. He could whip out just about anything you needed in an instant—flat triangles of different sizes and angles, templates with shaped cutouts, or a pointy scissors-like thing called a compass for drawing any size circle.

Having gotten everyone's attention, the teacher sat down again and began digging around in the stuff atop his desk, obviously trying to find something. Good luck with that! As usual, his desk was overflowing with plan-scrolls and small-scale models of temples, houses, and other buildings. In addition to teaching, he was famed for designing and building Zeus's temple in Olympia. There was a golden statue of Zeus inside it that was one of the Seven Wonders of the Ancient World!

On the wall behind Mr. Libon's chair were numerous hand-lettered signs with encouraging or funny slogans.

BE THE ARCHITECT OF YOUR BEST FUTURE.

BUILD FRIENDSHIPS.

ARCHITECTURE NEVER FALLS DOWN ON THE JOB.

IF YOU HIT A BRICK WALL, BUILD A DOOR THROUGH IT.

While the teacher was busy at his desk, Calliope leaned toward Medusa and quickly whispered, "If you want to come to my room after dinner tonight, I could give you some more ideas to choose from."

"Great," said Medusa, nodding eagerly. "I'll come, thanks."

Cool, thought Calliope. Tonight wasn't going to be all about Medusa's need for ideas, though. The unsuspecting snaky-haired girl didn't know that Calliope had recently decided to "interview" roommates. Because she didn't have one yet. And she'd heard that Medusa didn't either.

Calliope had been rooming by herself in the dorm ever since she'd arrived at MOA, and she didn't like it one bit. She missed her eight sisters—well, the seven who were not at the Academy, anyway. She still got to see her oldest sister, Muse Urania, almost daily since she taught Science-ology at the school. Unfortunately, sometimes Urania acted like she thought she was Calliope's mom. Urania was twenty-six years old, so she was fourteen years older than Calliope!

As Mr. Libon began to talk about the design projects that would be due next Wednesday—

individual projects they'd been working on since Calliope had first started at MOA—she shot Medusa a look.

Would the green-skinned girl make a good roommate? Hopefully, tonight's meeting would help Calliope decide. If it seemed like they'd be a good match, she could ask Medusa to sleep over sometime. She wasn't going to rush into anything. She wanted just the right person, someone who would be a good friend and not boss her around like Urania and some of her other sisters tended to do. They meant well, but hello? She wasn't a baby anymore.

She tuned back in to Mr. Libon just in time to hear him say, "Let's talk about how your projects are progressing. I want to hear a brief update from each of you, one by one."

Yikes! A flurry of panic swirled inside Calliope's

chest. She hoped he wouldn't call on her first. With luck, maybe the lyrebell would ring before he got to her. Because the thing was, she wasn't as far along on her project as she had hoped she would be by now.

Mr. Libon picked up a three-sided wooden ruler from his desk. He waved it in the air to emphasize certain points as he spoke to the class. "Remember that Principal Zeus and I will be choosing the most creative and interesting project design—for a temple, a house, or whatever—to actually be built." He paused, his eyes sweeping the students. "So now is your chance to get valuable feedback from others on your projects. Who would like to go first?"

Hands shot into the air. But Calliope's wasn't one of them. Sad to say, but as of today she still hadn't come up with a design! And that was news she didn't want to share, thank you very much.

Mr. Libon called on a godboy with blond hair and light turquoise skin named Poseidon. Grasping his planscroll, Poseidon stood. Then he strode confidently to the front of the room. *Snap!* With a flick of his wrist he unrolled the planscroll.

"I've designed a new water park," he said proudly. "It'll be as cool as the one I built in Athens but with even more slides, more fountains, and more pools." As he spoke, he pointed to places on his scroll where he planned to add the additional features. He'd used a spiral symbol to represent the slides, triangles to represent the fountains, and circles to represent the pools.

"Awesome!" a godboy named Dionysus exclaimed, pumping a fist in the air. Several other students also made noises of approval.

Poseidon grinned at them all. Then with a sideways

glance at Mr. Libon, he said, "If my design is chosen to be built, I'm going to name this new water park after my first one in Athens. I'll call it Poseidon Water Waves II."

Calliope had been to Poseidon's water park in Athens, and it was indeed fantastic, with gracefully curving slides made of polished marble, tons of fountains, and pools of turquoise water topped with lily pads. It also had real mermaids, mermen, and sea monsters! But it seemed to her that just adding more of the same kinds of features wouldn't be enough to make this new water park stand out.

"How about if you added some completely new features too?" she suggested enthusiastically. "Like an underwater cave, maybe? The walls could be lit from below with magical colored lights!"

"Hey, great idea, Calliope," Poseidon said. "Thanks!"

Mr. Libon smiled at her. "Excellent." Then he glanced around the room. "Does anyone else have feedback for Poseidon?"

It seemed that no one did, or maybe they were all just anxious for their turns to speak. If students did have a project ready, it was a good idea to get a critique now. Just in case their plan was a dud or had drawbacks they were unaware of.

Poseidon sat down, and Mr. Libon called on Amphitrite next. Her desk was right in front of Calliope's. As Amphitrite stepped with her plan-scroll to the front of the room, Calliope thought how hard it would be for anyone to guess that the turquoise-haired girl was a Nereid—a nymph of the sea. After all, most of the time she was at MOA, she walked around on two legs. When she was in water, though, her gold-colored chiton transformed into a golden-scaled tail and she became a mergirl. Calliope had seen it happen during a swim night at the Academy pool a week ago.

Like Calliope, Amphitrite hadn't been at MOA for long. Long enough to have a crush, though, judging from the smiles she and Poseidon traded in class all the time. Calliope planted her elbow on her desktop, set her chin in her palm, and thought wistfully of Homer again as Amphitrite began to speak.

The sea nymph's planscroll showed detailed sketches for a landscaping project—a lush and beautiful undersea garden. "I designed it to surround a golden palace at the bottom of the Aegean Sea," Amphitrite told the class in her bubbly voice.

"A palace being built in my honor by inhabitants of the sea," Poseidon interrupted her to boast.

Amphitrite smiled at him. *Again.* As godboy of the sea, Poseidon saw to the welfare of all sea creatures, so it made sense that they would build a palace in his honor. And Calliope could understand why he would be proud of it.

"Right," Amphitrite went on. "My family and other residents of the watery realms are hard at work on the palace. I've designed my garden in five triangular sections. The sections form a star shape with the palace at the center, and each section will feature a different type of garden."

Pointing to each of the triangular sections in turn, she described the plants that would populate each of the five garden areas. She'd planned a coral garden, a garden dominated by various sea grasses, a rock garden designed to look like a series of tide pools, a garden of brightly colored plants and simple animals such as sea cucumbers, and a garden with a treasure chest theme that included sand dollars and oysters with pearls.

Poseidon started clapping the minute she'd finished. "Pure genius!" he proclaimed admiringly.

I'd give anything to have Homer speak so highly of me, thought Calliope. However such admiring words had never passed his lips—not headed in her direction, anyway.

"I love your concept of five gardens in one," Calliope said to Amphitrite. "But I wonder if you need something to link them all together. Like a border outlining the star's shape?"

"Oh! Yeah, like a little fence of greenery or shells. That's an interesting idea," said Amphitrite. "I'll definitely think about it!"

Several other students gave suggestions this time too, including Medusa. She thought a garden with a sea snake and eel habitat might be nice. Her snakes bobbed their heads in agreement.

When the period ended without Calliope being asked to share her (as yet nonexistent) project, she jumped up in relief. She grabbed her schoolbag and headed for the door.

"Just a minute, Calliope," Mr. Libon called to her before she could exit the room. "I'd like to speak with you."

Calliope froze in her tracks and swung back around to look at him. "Um. Okay," she said. Feeling nervous about what he could want, she went up to his desk and stood there fiddling with her bag. She had decorated it with the names of famous epic poets, such as Hesiod, Asius of Samos, Eumelus of

Corinth, Panyassis, and—most important—*Homer.*

She relaxed a little when Mr. Libon smiled at her. "I really appreciate the great feedback and suggestions you give others in class," he began.

"Thanks," she said, relaxing even more. "It's easy for me. Being a Muse and all." As Muses, she and her eight sisters served as sources of inspiration to others for all kinds of creativity in the arts and sciences.

Mr. Libon nodded. "Thing is," he went on, "I'm concerned that I've heard nothing from you so far about the project *you're* working on." Eyeing her keenly, he picked up a protractor shaped like a flat semicircle, poked one finger through its open middle, and began absentmindedly twirling it around. "What can you tell me about it?"

Calliope gulped. "Well, it's kind of hard to explain right now," she said. Then, hoping to fool him into thinking she had a solid start on her project, she waved her hands around enthusiastically while describing a temple-like structure. "It'll have all kinds of ornate columns with flowered vines wound around them, gold statues of various gods and goddesses, amazing fountains that spray fifty feet into the air, and . . . just about anything you could ever want, really."

Mr. Libon cocked his head. "And what's your building's purpose going to be?" he asked. "What and who is it intended for?"

"For . . . for anyone who likes awesome buildings!" Calliope answered, smiling brightly.

"I don't suppose you have a planscroll for this *awesome building*, do you?" Mr. Libon asked. He gestured at her schoolbag.

Calliope thought about lying. She could have said that she'd left the planscroll in her dorm room or her locker. But somehow she just couldn't do it. "Uh, not yet," she told Mr. Libon truthfully. "The ideas part is easy for me. I've always got a ton of ideas, but choosing between them is hard," she admitted. "I'm always worried that some better idea will come along. So I hate to narrow it down, you know?"

"I do understand," Mr. Libon said sympathetically. "But as *you* know, your project is due on Wednesday, and it's worth eighty percent of your grade. You haven't got that much time. So my advice to you is to choose the idea or ideas that appeal to you most right now and go with them. That's what architects do in the end. A bunch of amazing ideas that aren't ever put to paper will never a building make." He paused and scribbled down the words he'd just said, probably planning to make another handwritten sign for his wall.

When he'd finished writing, he glanced at her

again. "Muse Urania is your older sister, isn't that right?" he asked.

Calliope nodded. "I've got eight older sisters. But she's the oldest."

Mr. Libon's brow furrowed. "Do you think it might help if the three of us got together to talk about the trouble you're having getting going on this project?"

"What? No!" Calliope exclaimed, shaking her head so hard that her ponytail almost came undone. The last thing she needed was to have her sister nosing around in her life. She loved Urania, and her other sisters too. But despite the fact that Calliope was twelve years old now, they still treated her like she was five most of the time. In other words, they were a little too into her business.

"She's superbusy right now with, um, *stuff.* I wouldn't want to bother her about this. Anyway, I've got it under control," she added by way of explanation. "I'll take care of it."

"Okay," Mr. Libon said after a moment's hesitation. "But if you change your mind and feel like you need some help, just tell me. I'm sure your sister would be happy to find time to meet with us."

"Oh, sure. Yeah. I will," Calliope assured him, starting to ease toward the doorway. But all the while she was thinking, *Not a chance!*

At last she reached the exit. "Okay, well, thanks, Mr. Libon." She ducked out fast. Once through the doorway, she breathed a sigh of relief. Out in the hallway a sense of determination filled her. The very minute she got to her dorm room, she was going to sit down at her desk. She'd let nothing stop her from getting this project going. For real this time. She was going to narrow down her ideas to the very best one and get started on a design for a house or a temple or whatever.

She didn't really care if her design was the one chosen to be built, she thought as she started down the hall. Her goal at this point was simply to get the project done so she could pass Architecture-ology with a decent grade. Because if her sisters ever found out that she was struggling in a class, they'd forever be checking up on her. And more than anything else, she wanted to stand on her own two feet, to have them see her as the almost-teenager she was!

2
Pros and Cons

BEFORE CALLIOPE COULD START UP THE MARBLE staircase to the girls' dorm on the fourth floor, she heard shouts coming from outside. Curious as to what was going on, she veered toward MOA's bronze front doors instead. *What could it hurt if I began my project a few minutes later than planned?* Calliope thought as she pushed out through the doors.

A ring of godboys and mortal boys that included

Heracles, Ares, and Hades was gathered in the court-yard below. In the middle of the ring stood the god-boy Apollo and a satyr named Marsyas, who was half boy and half goat, with pointy ears, two small horns on his head, goat legs, and a goat tail. As she paused at the top of the steps and looked down, she over-heard Marsyas challenge Apollo to a battle.

"Yes!" Ares, the godboy of war, cheered upon hearing this.

"Not the kind with spears and weapons," Marsyas informed him. "The kind with notes. Specifically, a *musical* battle."

"Huh?" said Ares. He wasn't the only one who looked confused. Calliope was too. What did Marsyas have in mind?

"We'll battle it out at the music festival. You know, down on Earth in Greece tomorrow at the Theatre of Dionysus in Athens," Marsyas told Apollo. "Sort of like a battle of the bands, only with just us two musicians."

While he spoke, the satyr ran a hand over the sleek black-and-white goat-hair vest he always wore. It was common knowledge that this vest was his prize possession, made from his very own hair by the nymph Echo, a skilled clothing designer. He was as proud of it as the phenomenally strong mortal boy Heracles was of the lion-skin cape he wore everywhere. Did Marsyas hope it would bring him luck against Apollo?

Like most everyone, Calliope already knew about the upcoming festival. In fact, she was going to be singing in it with her eight sister Muses. She loved singing—any type of artistic expression, really—but she dreaded the questions her sisters were sure to ask when they got together. *How are your classes going?*

Need any help with them or with anything else? Are you making friends at MOA? Got a roommate yet? Have you been invited to sit with Aphrodite and her friends at lunch?

Duh, right. *Not.* Because goddessgirls like Aphrodite already had a million friends! Sure, that popular goddessgirl was nice to Calliope and had already made a point of welcoming her to MOA. Same went for Aphrodite's equally popular BFFs, Athena, Persephone, and Artemis.

But Calliope was looking for a special friend with lots of time to hang out with *her.* There was an art to making friends, in her humble opinion. You didn't just push yourself onto random people. You first got acquainted with them, got to know them bit by bit, and then made your move. However, in the meantime her room was feeling very lonely. She had even started talking to her pillows at times!

Dark-haired Apollo eyed Marsyas. "You? Against me? In a music battle? Are you *sure* you want to do this?" Apollo was godboy of music, as well as the godboy of truth and prophecy. Everyone knew he was awesome at playing a stringed instrument called the lyre.

For his part, Marsyas was an awesome player of the aulos. It was a double-piped reed instrument that had been invented by Principal Zeus's daughter, the superbrainy goddessgirl Athena. Rumor had it that Marsyas's favorite aulos was one Athena had tossed out after several students at MOA had remarked on how her cheeks bulged when she played. Calliope found the rumor hard to believe, though. Athena didn't seem that vain about her appearance. More likely Marsyas had come by the aulos some other way. Maybe Athena had even given it to him.

"Sure I'm sure," Marsyas said. Grinning big, he did a little impromptu jig, his hooves stamping against the courtyard's marble tiles. "So prepare to get beat, lyre-boy. You are going *down!*"

Ye gods, thought Calliope. That was no way to talk to a godboy. Immortals were supposed to be treated with respect. Otherwise they might become angry and vengeful. If Marsyas weren't careful, he could wind up in serious hot water. Of course that particular situation would be most likely to happen if he made Poseidon, the godboy of the *sea*, mad. With Apollo, he'd wind up in seriously *note*-able trouble, though!

Luckily for Marsyas, Apollo kept a cool head now and only grinned, saying, "You wish! You are *sooo* doomed, satyr."

"What's the prize going to be? For the winner, I mean," asked Ares.

"The satisfaction of being proved best," Marsyas said smugly. "Plus, the loser has to fork over whatever prize the winner wants, no complaints."

At this, Apollo seemed to hesitate, which surprised Calliope. Because why would the godboy of music care what would happen to the loser in this battle? No way could Apollo lose!

When Ares nudged him, Apollo quickly grinned. "All right, Marsyas. You're on. And you'd better watch out!"

The group of boys broke up and began to move in different directions, all excitedly discussing what had just happened. Remembering her project, Calliope determinedly went back inside the Academy.

"Hey, wait up! Yoo-hoo!" someone called to her as she started upstairs to her room. A girl with spiky orange hair and small orange wings at her back fluttered over. It was Pheme, the goddessgirl of gossip.

"Could you help me?" Pheme asked after she'd caught up to Calliope on the stairs. As usual, her words puffed from her orange-glossed lips to rise above her head in little cloud-letters, before fading away. Those cloud-letters were a useful gift that guaranteed her words would spread swiftly whenever others were around to see them.

"The deadline for my next gossip column in *Teen Scrollazine* is tomorrow," Pheme went on. She sounded a little frantic. "And right now I only have one solid item. I need at least one more idea—fast! Two, if possible. Can you help? Got a little inspiration to spare maybe?"

Calliope shrugged uncertainly as Pheme climbed the stairs with her. "I don't really know much about the gossip . . . er . . . news around here." At times like this Calliope almost wished her fellow students didn't know she was a Muse. She really needed to get going on her Architecture-ology project! But then she realized that she did have something she could share. So she told Pheme about tomorrow's festival.

"Oh, thanks. I'd forgotten about that," said Pheme. "I need details, though. You and your sisters will be singing in it, right?"

Calliope nodded as they reached the second floor. "Yes, and I just heard that Marsyas and Apollo are going to have a musical battle at the festival."

"Ooh! Really?" Pheme licked her lips, her eyes shining with excitement now. "That's perfect! Tell me more," she pleaded. So as they continued up to the fourth floor, Calliope told her everything she'd overheard just minutes before.

"Thanks mega-much," Pheme said at last. "That's a real scoop!"

"You're welcome," said Calliope. "So what was the news you already had?" she asked, curious.

"Oh, it's one-and-a-half-week-old news, really," Pheme said. "About the stolen Hero-ology classroom game pieces."

In the act of pushing through the door into the girls' dorm hall, Calliope froze to look back at Pheme. "*Stolen?* For real? I mean, I thought they were just *missing*, as in misplaced."

"Nope. Stolen," Pheme affirmed as they entered the hall. "I was in the office this morning and over-heard Mr. Cyclops tell Principal Zeus that at first he thought someone at MOA had hidden the game pieces as a prank. He felt sure they'd be returned in a day or two. But since they haven't been, now he thinks they were kidnapped!"

After saying this, she reached above her head and quickly brushed away her cloud-letters, even though no one else was around in the dorm right then to read them.

"Whoa!" Calliope exclaimed. She turned the knob on the door to her room and nudged the door open with one shoulder. "So, nobody has any idea who took them?"

Pheme shook her head. "Nuh-uh. But keep this conversation to yourself till the scrollazine is out, okay?" she said before brushing away her cloud-words again. "I want to be the one to spread the news."

"Sure," said Calliope.

Distracted by the sound of another door opening, Pheme turned her head to look down the hall. Her eyes lit up at what she'd spotted. Calliope leaned back from the doorway to see Aphrodite coming toward them, holding her sweet black-and-white kitten, Adonis. The kitten was wearing an adorable little tunic edged in gold that matched the one Aphrodite was wearing.

"Wow. I have got to ask her about those matching outfits—might be another good item for my column," Pheme murmured. With a quick wave, she dashed off to intercept Aphrodite, calling over her shoulder to Calliope, "Thanks a bunch for the help! And good luck in the festival!"

Hmm. Aphrodite rooms alone, Calliope thought as she shut herself inside her room. So did Pheme, for that matter. Roommate possibilities? She'd have to think about it.

Once inside, Calliope found a note that had

been slipped under her door. It was from her sister Urania. *Don't forget to practice our new song,* the note said. Calliope frowned in annoyance. Her sisters were always giving her little prods, "helpful" tips, and gentle reminders like this one. As if she weren't old enough to figure out for herself what she needed to do!

It didn't help that within their chosen areas of expertise, her eight older sisters were all mega-high-achieving and successful. Urania was not only an inspiring teacher but a well-respected amateur astronomer. Clio was a historian. Melpomene wrote tragedies, and Thalia, comedies. Euterpe played flute in an orchestra in Olympia, and also wrote lyric poetry. Erato wrote poems about love, while Polyhymnia's poems were of a more spiritual nature. And Terpsichore, who was Calliope's favorite sister because she was kind and gentle and hardly ever nagged, was a fabulous dancer who performed all over Greece.

Having such amazingly accomplished sisters meant that Calliope had a lot to live up to. But did their successes give them the right to try to run her life too?

"Anyway, I can't practice my song right now because I've got something else to do," she informed the note, as if it were actually her sister. "Namely, stop myself from flunking Architecture-ology!" Not that she'd ever really voice that last thing to her sister, mind you.

She wadded up Urania's note and tossed it into a high arc. *Thunk!* It landed in her trash can to join several others sent to her just yesterday by various sisters.

Settling at her desk, she took out a sheet of papyrus and a feather pen. Calliope had at least a dozen pens scattered around her room—attached to the door, on shelves above her bed, even inside her closet—so that she'd always have one close at hand whenever inspiration struck. If she didn't write ideas down, she often forgot them when they were crowded out by other, newer ideas that came into her mind.

The first thing she needed to do, of course, was to decide what kind of building she wanted to design for her project. Mr. Libon was right about one thing. Until she made up her mind about that, she couldn't really get started.

She began by scribbling a list of ideas. Then beside each she wrote the pros and cons of choosing that particular idea. Her list included temples, houses, coliseums, gymnasiums, and more. Unfortunately, she wasn't all that excited about any of the possibilities she'd come up with so far. Her mind wandered and she started to imagine more unusual project ideas.

While staring at her feather pen, an image of a building made of feathers shaped like a nest popped into her head. Possibly a birdbrained idea, but you never knew. She jotted the idea down.

Or maybe she could design a house sort of like her childhood home on the slopes of Mount Helicon, which stood in a meadow with freshwater springs. Only, this new house would have a turf roof seeded with flowers. It could be built up on stilts and have a spring flowing under it.

Before she knew it, she was off and running with new ideas, completely abandoning her pros and cons list. Soon she had jotted down twenty-five all-new project possibilities. These included a tall building shaped like a thunderbolt, a mobile chariot-racing arena that could move from city to city on a cloud, and a store selling winged sandals that was shaped like a giant foot. *Godsamighty!* Every time she tried to rein in her mind, it reacted like a wild horse, breaking free from restraints and racing away. It was like her mind had a mind of its own!

She tossed aside her pen in frustration and got up from her desk. Movement often helped to clear her head, so she began to pace the narrow aisle that divided her room in two. Each side had a bed, a closet, and a desk, but Calliope was only using the left half of the room since she had no roommate—yet.

Until she'd come to MOA, she'd always thought she'd *like* not having to share sleeping space the way she had with her sisters back home. There she'd shared with different sisters at different times, rotating around over the years as they were growing up.

Here in the dorm she'd quickly discovered that she didn't like rooming alone. Recently she'd invited a girl named Aglaia from her first-period Music-ology class to spend the night with her. They'd had a great time together chatting and laughing. Calliope had kind of been hoping they might become roommates, but then she'd found out that Aglaia already had a roommate—the goddessgirl of the hearth, Hestia.

Too bad! Not the end of the world, though. There were other girls without roommates, such as Medusa and Aphrodite. Pheme, too.

Calliope plopped onto her bed, picked up her flower-shaped pillow, and spoke to the smiley face in its yellow center. "But to tell you the truth, as much as I like that goddessgirl of gossip, I don't think we'd want to room with her, do you?"

She turned the pillow back and forth in her hands

so that it seemed to be shaking its head. "Yeah, exactly. I'd feel like I'd need to take care in everything I said so it wouldn't get repeated in cloud-letters to every-one at MOA," she told it.

Hugging the pillow, Calliope gazed at the right half of her room. She had made up the extra bed with some of the school's linens when Aglaia had come to spend the night. The plain white comforter, which was still on the bed, was stamped with an MOA logo and a thunderbolt—Principal Zeus's sym-bol. Otherwise, she'd left that side of her room empty and bare, including the walls. When she did find a roommate (and she kept telling herself it was only a matter of time), her roomie would want to decorate to her own taste.

Calliope flopped onto her side and sank into her own plush comforter, a cheerful yellow one that was decorated with black staff lines and musical notes. A gift from Terpsichore. She wished she could find a roomie just like her favorite sister. A roomie she could feel comfortable exchanging confidences with.

The comforter was an unintentional reminder that she still needed to practice the new song she and her sisters would be singing tomorrow. Oh, there was just so much she needed to do! Merely thinking about it all made her feel tired. She rolled to lie on her back and stared up at the wall next to her bed.

She'd covered the wall with quotations from writers and artists she had inspired to create great works. In addition to Homer, they included the famous sculptor Pygmalion and the pop star Orpheus. She'd had a direct influence on the lyrics of one of Orpheus's most recent hit songs, "You A-Muse Me." Locating the first line of the song high on the wall, she sang it out loud in a lilting soprano voice, "You a-Muse me, confuse me. . . . O, will your heart bruise meee-ee-ee?"

Now her gaze went to the autographed picture of Homer on the wall at the end of her bed. He'd given her the painting on the day *The Odyssey* had been published. An inscription at the bottom read: *To my Muse, with cheers and thanks!*

No matter how many other creative mortals she inspired, Homer was the only one she'd ever crushed on. So it wasn't like she was boy crazy. There was just something about Homer that made her adore him. Unfortunately, like her sisters, he seemed to think she was a baby. Or a little kid, anyway.

Calliope sighed. Someday she'd like to achieve lasting fame that wasn't attached to another's name. Maybe then others would finally see her as grown up!

Thinking about being grown up made her realize

that, once again, she'd lost her focus. If she weren't more careful, she really would flunk Architecture-ology. And that would be horrible. She liked being here at MOA, even if she was sometimes lonely. She was grateful that Urania had gone to bat for her to convince Principal Zeus to issue her an invitation to attend.

Calliope was sure she was worthy of that invitation. She'd just never had to prove herself before like this. Staying on task and studying would be a lot easier with a friend, aka a roommate. Not to lean on or anything, but for companionship and to have a good role model nearby. When her roomie studied, she would study too. Just like she'd done with her sisters back home.

"Don't worry. We'll get a roommate soon, Flowerface," she told the pillow in a confident voice.

"But for now it's just you and me. Well . . . back to my Architecture-ology project."

Hopping up, she set the pillow on the empty bed opposite her own. Then, reluctantly, she returned to her desk.

3

All About Muses

BY DINNERTIME CALLIOPE HAD MANAGED TO narrow her list of possible Architecture-ology projects to just five. She'd thrown out her most boring ideas and also the most far-fetched (such as the mobile chariot-racing arena that could travel by cloud). It was progress, even if she wasn't wildly excited about developing a planscroll for any of the remaining five.

She returned to her room after dinner, determined

to go over the tunes and lyrics for the three songs she and her eight sisters would be singing at the music festival the next day. Two of the songs she already knew well, since she and her sisters had sung them many times at other events. But she hadn't yet memorized the tune and lyrics for the new song.

She should have begun learning it earlier. Urania had tried to get Calliope to practice with her all week. But Calliope had put her sister off, saying she was too busy with homework to get together. She'd told Urania she'd practice on her own. She hadn't, though.

Her excuse had been at least partly true. But she also resented Urania's constant attempts to arrange joint practice sessions. It made Calliope feel like she was being bossed around. And that made her rebel. She didn't *need* guidance on every little thing, for godness' sake!

She began to warm up her vocal cords. She was in the midst of singing a song called "Knock, Knock, Knocking on Zeus's Door"—a song she and her sisters often sang at concerts, though it wouldn't be on tomorrow's program—when someone knocked on her door.

"Come, come, coming to answer my-y door," she sang out as she went to open the door. She was surprised to see Medusa standing just outside. But then she remembered that she had invited the snaky-haired girl to drop by to talk about ideas for her Revenge-ology paper.

"Oh! Come in," she said at last.

Medusa must have sensed her surprise. In an uncertain tone she asked, "You *were* expecting me, right?"

"Yes, definitely," Calliope replied brightly. This

was going to be a great opportunity to get to know this mortal girl better. And if they got along well, she'd ask Medusa if she'd be interested in becoming roommates. Easy-peasy.

"Pleasey. Oh, I mean, *please come in and sit*," she said, gesturing toward her spare bed as Medusa came into her room.

After Calliope closed the door, she and Medusa took seats across from each other on the two beds. "How's it going?" Calliope asked. Her eyes traveled to the top of Medusa's head, noticing that her snakes were all wearing sparkly green ribbons around their "necks." "Those guys look so cute, all dressed up!" she added.

The snakes responded by standing a little taller. Medusa smiled wide. "Want to know their names?"

Calliope hadn't realized they had names. Who

named their hair? But then, these snakes were obviously *pets*. "Sure."

Pointing to each snake in turn, Medusa began calling out their names. "Viper, Flicka, Pretzel, Snapper, Twister, Slinky, Lasso, Slither, Scaly, Emerald, Sweetpea, and Wiggle." In turn each snake bobbed its head at Calliope in a little bow of greeting. How gentle and sweet they were!

"Happy to meet you," she told them, doing a little bow in return.

"So I've thought about those ideas you gave me earlier for my Revenge-ology paper," Medusa said, getting straight to the point. "And I really like the one about interviewing other students about times when they've taken revenge on someone."

"Oh," Calliope said. "Are you sure? I could probably come up with several more ideas that might be even—"

"Don't bother," interrupted Medusa. "I've made up my mind. In fact, I've already started my interviews." As she spoke, she pulled a little sack from her pocket. There was a label on it that read, SNAKE SNACKS. "My snakes are hungry. Mind if I feed them while we talk?" she asked. "I'd like to interview *you* for my paper too."

"Go right ahead," Calliope said. She couldn't believe how little time it had taken Medusa to decide which idea she wanted to pursue for her paper. Seemed like she'd want to consider more alternatives. On the other hand, Calliope thought, if *she* could make choices as quickly, her Architecture-ology project might already be finished!

"So have you ever taken revenge on someone?" Medusa asked as she scooped a handful of what looked like dried peas and carrots from the little sack. She tossed them into the air. *Snap! Snap! Snap!* Her snakes gobbled them down in seconds.

Watching them, Calliope thought about the question. "Not all on my own, but my sisters and I did take revenge on the Sirens once. There were three of them. Odd-looking, wicked creatures. Women from the waist up and birds from the waist down, you know?"

"Yeah. I know about them. Their favorite pastime is using their beautiful voices to lure sailing ships toward the rocks where they perch at sea. The ships crash on the rocks and the sailors drown. So what did you do to them? Revenge-wise, I mean," said Medusa.

"Well," Calliope went on, "what happened was—"

"Wait a second," Medusa interrupted. "I need to take some notes." She shoved the snake snack sack back inside her pocket. Then she seemed to search inside it for something more. Coming up empty, she said, "Rats. I forgot my Revenge-ology notescroll. Can you come down to my room?"

"Yeah!" Calliope jumped at the chance to learn more about this girl by seeing her room. *Literally* jumped. She leaped off her bed and tossed the music-scroll she'd been practicing with onto her desk. Medusa looked a little surprised at her enthusiasm, but then led her down the hall. Once they were in Medusa's room, they sat in her two desk chairs.

Not wanting to seem too nosy, Calliope surveyed the room in one sweeping glance. Almost everything of Medusa's was green. She had matching green polka-dotted bedspreads, a green rug, and except for one curiously bright gold one, all of the chitons sticking out of the open closet were some shade of green too.

A bulletin board over one bed held random

stuff, such as a dried bouquet of purple flowers, some Oracle-O cookie fortunes, and a purple scroll with a heart on the outside. The purple stuff was probably from Dionysus, her crush. It was a color he seemed to favor. On the shelf above one of the desks was a small amount of makeup—green lip gloss and glittery green nail polish. The room's decor was simple and cute, she decided. Also, the room was not too messy and not too tidy. Calliope's hopes about the two girls rooming together rose.

"Okay. Go on. The Sirens," Medusa prompted. Her pen was poised above a scroll unfurled on her desk.

"Oh yeah. Basically, it all started when the Sirens lost a singing contest to me and my sisters." Calliope ran a hand over her wavy red ponytail, remembering. "That would have been the end of things, but instead of being good sports about it, those birdbrained women tried to claim we'd cheated. Bribed the judges or something. So we . . ." She paused, a little embarrassed. "Are you sure you want to hear this? It's history now. And I was only six."

"You can't leave me hanging. Tell me!" said Medusa, sounding intrigued. As she leaned forward, so did her snakes.

"Well, just to teach them a lesson, we plucked out some of their feathers!" said Calliope. "They were grounded till they grew more and could fly again."

"Ha!" said Medusa, scribbling away on her note-scroll. "Good one. Served them right! Everyone knows goddesses and gods expect to be honored and don't take kindly to creatures who show them disrespect."

When Medusa had finished writing, she shut her

notescroll and tossed her pen down. Then she rose as if ready to escort Calliope out. "Well, thanks."

"So!" said Calliope, hoping to delay her. She needed more information before she could properly rate this girl as a prospective roomie. "Heard any good revenge stories from other immortals yet?"

Medusa nodded and sat back down. "My favorite is how Athena turned a mortal girl into a spider."

"Oh yeah. I heard something about that," said Calliope. "Her name was Arachne?"

"Right," said Medusa, grinning. "She was rude to Athena after challenging her to a weaving contest, and then made things even worse by creating a tapestry that was insulting to Zeus."

"In what way?" Calliope asked, curious.

"Athena wouldn't say," said Medusa. "But rumor has it that the tapestry showed Zeus hopping around in pain with a thunderbolt stuck in his foot and the hem of his tunic on fire."

Calliope gasped. "No wonder Athena took revenge!"

Insulting immortals was never smart. And challenging them to contests wasn't usually a good idea either. In fact, that satyr Marsyas would have been wise to think about that before challenging Apollo to tomorrow's musical battle.

Calliope smiled at Medusa. And her snakes, too. She thought they all might be a good fit. Maybe it was time to try a sleepover. But before she could suggest one, Medusa asked abruptly, "So, what's it like being a Muse? Do you have, like, special powers?"

"Besides the ability to inspire, you mean?" said Calliope.

Medusa nodded.

Calliope furrowed her brow, thinking. "Well, my

sisters and I can cast spells, just like other immortals," she said. "But that's about it, really. And our ability to inspire is limited to our areas of expertise."

"That's what I thought," said Medusa. "By the way, I love *The Odyssey*." Suddenly, she jumped up and spread her arms wide. Until that moment, her snakes had been quiet, either bored with the conversation or maybe just sleepy after eating their snacks. They'd curled themselves into a tight bun at the back of her neck.

But now they began wriggling as Medusa quoted from *The Odyssey* in a dramatic voice: "*My word, how mortals take the gods to task! All their afflictions come from us, we hear. And what of their own failings? Greed and folly double the suffering in the lot of man.*"

"Those are my favorite lines!" Calliope exclaimed in delight.

"Did you tell them to Homer so he could write them down?" Medusa asked bluntly, sitting cross-legged on her bed now and waving Calliope over to sit on the opposite bed.

"Well . . ." As Calliope stood, she knocked a couple of scrolls off the desk she'd been sitting near. When she picked them up, one of them unrolled to reveal some cute drawings. "Hey! I just remembered you're a writer, aren't you? And an artist. I read in *Teen Scrollazine* that some of your comics won a contest a while back. They were about a character called the Queen of Mean, right? That's mega-cool!" Since Medusa was a writer and Calliope inspired writers, they were beginning to seem more and more like a good roomie fit! Excitement rose higher in her.

"Thanks, but I promise I wasn't asking how you'd helped Homer because I wanted help for my comics,"

Medusa assured her confidently. "I'm just curious about how this inspiration thing works."

"Well, it's not an exact science," Calliope explained, setting the comicscrolls aside to go sit on the edge of the spare bed. "Every artist or author I inspire already has the talent inside him or her. I just try to bring it out and help them when they're stumped. As I recall, what I said to Homer was actually something like this: 'Mortals are so unfair to the gods. They think everything bad comes from us. They're not perfect, you know. They bring a lot of bad stuff down on their own heads through their greediness and foolishness.'"

"Hmm," said Medusa. "Same idea, but your words don't have quite the same ring to them as Homer's."

"I agree. He's *amazing*," Calliope said with heartfelt enthusiasm. In her view Homer deserved every scrap of praise he got for his books, even if she had inspired them. She was just pleased to have helped him.

Medusa lifted an eyebrow. "So I saw that stuff about Homer in your room. Are you, like, crushing on him?" she asked in her straightforward way.

Calliope felt herself blush. "No!" she lied quickly.

As if sensing the lie, Medusa sent her a doubting look. Ignoring it, Calliope traced a finger around a polka dot on Medusa's bedcover. She wondered if she should reconsider Medusa's suitability as a roommate.

"Okay, well . . . ," said Medusa, standing to usher Calliope out.

Would this girl make a good roommate? Calliope wondered again. She was pretty blunt. And if her snakes hissed at night, it might be hard to sleep. But Medusa and her snakes were also interesting and fun. Plus, Medusa appreciated Homer's writing just like Calliope did.

"You know, Ms. Hydra never assigned me a room-mate," Calliope said, deciding to sidle up to the topic. This had probably just been an oversight on the part of Zeus's nine-headed administrative assistant. Still, Calliope wanted to choose her own roommate now that she had the chance. That way, she'd get someone well suited.

"Lucky you," said Medusa, sitting back on her bed again. Her snakes had curled up into that bun again, Calliope noticed.

"Isn't it great having a room to yourself?" Medusa continued. "When I started at MOA back in third grade, Pandora was my roommate. I like her, but her constant questions drove me crazy. So I started answering all her questions with more questions, till she asked for a new room assignment." Medusa grinned. "She's Athena's problem now."

"Oh," said Calliope. She hadn't known till now that Medusa had once had a roommate.

"Then Ms. Hydra assigned Pheme to room with me," Medusa went on. "I know she couldn't help it, but her word-puffing habit drove me even crazier than Pandora's questions had. I finally declared our room a no-smoking zone. Since that meant she couldn't talk, she eventually moved out too."

"I see," said Calliope, wondering if she had some annoying habit that she wasn't aware of. If so, she might not fare any better as Medusa's roommate than Pheme or Pandora had.

Right then and there Calliope abandoned the idea of asking this girl to share a room. Even though Medusa hadn't actually said so, it seemed obvious that she was not in the market for a roommate. Calliope would just have to find someone else to ask!

4

Fun and Games

SUDDENLY SHOUTS CAME FROM THE COURTYARD below Medusa's dorm window. She and Calliope rushed to gaze outside. Some students had gathered to play games and toss balls around. Dionysus was among them.

"Yeah! A hang-out session. C'mon!" said Medusa. She dashed for the door, then looked back at Calliope with a question in her eyes. "You coming?"

Calliope hesitated, thinking of the sheet music back in her room. "Well . . . I *should* work on memorizing the new song lyrics for tomorrow's festival. And on my Architecture-ology project too." Then she grinned. "But playing games would be more fun."

"You know it!" said Medusa. "Besides, you've got tonight and the morning for memorizing the music. And even more time for homework."

Allowing herself to be convinced, Calliope nodded. "You're right. Let's go!" After all, this could be a great opportunity to size up other possible roommate candidates!

Outside, on a section of lawn that sloped down toward the sports fields, the students had started up a competitive game of Episkyros. It was a two-team ball game. A white middle line on the ground called the "skuros" separated the two teams, and there was another white goal line some distance behind each team. The object for each team was to pass the ball back and forth until one member was able to carry it over the opposing team's goal line.

Seeing Calliope and Medusa, Dionysus waved to them from one of the Episkyros teams that was currently forming. "Come help us beat these guys!" he shouted, gesturing at the other team.

"No way that's going to happen!" yelled Ares. He was on the opposing side.

At the same time Aphrodite, Artemis, and Amphitrite spotted the two girls. "Medusa! Calliope! Over here!" they shouted from a section of lawn bordering the courtyard. "We need more people for Ostrakinda!"

Ostrakinda was a game that also pitted two teams against each other. One team was called Night, and the other, Day. To begin, a single cockleshell was thrown to the ground. It was painted black on one side for night, and white on the opposite side for day. If a team's color landed faceup, they had to chase the other team until they were able to tag out one player. Then the shell was thrown again. The game went on like that until all of the players on one team had been tagged out.

"I'm going to go play Episkyros," Medusa said to Calliope. "How about you?"

"Ostrakinda for me," Calliope said. "I *love* that game." What she'd said was true, but she also had an ulterior motive. She really wanted to become friendlier with the three girls who'd called to them. Since Aphrodite, Artemis, and Amphitrite each roomed alone, any one of them could be a potential, perfect roommate!

"Okay. Later, then," said Medusa. As the snaky-haired girl ran off, Calliope jogged over to join the Ostrakinda game.

"Thanks for picking us instead of Episkyros," golden-haired Aphrodite said. Her blue eyes twinkled as she smiled at Calliope.

Calliope returned her smile with a teasing one. "No problem! But you'd better watch out if we end up on opposite teams. I'm pretty good. I played a lot of Ostrakinda with my sisters when we were growing up."

"An expert! You're on my team, then," Artemis yelled to her, overhearing. She was really into sports and competitions.

Six more girls were quickly recruited to make two five-member teams. Calliope, Athena, Aglaia, Amphitrite, and Artemis ended up together on the Day team, while Aphrodite, Persephone, Hestia, Pandora, and Pheme formed the Night team.

"Ready, everybody?" Amphitrite called out, holding up the painted shell.

"Ready!" they all yelled.

Calliope crouched, ready to run.

"Here we go, then!" Amphitrite tossed the shell high into the air in the middle of the girls.

It landed on the lawn, white side up.

"White!" Artemis called to Calliope and the rest of the Day team. "That's us!"

The girls all squealed in glee as the Day team members chased after the Night team members. Calliope chased Pandora, but that girl turned out to be curiously fast, and Calliope never could quite catch her.

"Score!" yelled Artemis after she'd tagged Hestia.

"Argh! My goose is cooked!" Hestia called out good-naturedly. She headed off to the designated "out" zone. There she sat atop the short stone wall bordering a fountain that featured several golden dolphins. Water spouted from their half-open mouths to fall into a broad pool at the base of the fountain behind her.

As they all regrouped for the next toss, everyone laughed at Hestia's turn of phrase because that girl was a *superb* cook. Pheme had even interviewed her about her recipes and stuff for *Teen Scrollazine*. It turned out that Hestia had created many of the dishes on the school's menu, such as yambrosia stew, celestial salad, and nectaroni. Lucky Aglaia. With Hestia as her roommate, she probably scored all kinds of leftover snacks Hestia brought back to their room from the cafeteria!

On the next toss the shell fell black side up. The Night team would do the chasing this time.

Hestia leaped to her feet from the fountain wall. Cheering her team members on, she yelled. "Go get 'em, Night. Run!"

As the Night team came after them, Calliope sprinted away to avoid being tagged. Luckily, she was a fast runner. But Aphrodite was also fast and was catching up. In the nick of time, Calliope swerved and darted, eluding her. Seconds later Persephone tagged out a different Day team member though—Athena.

"Who invented this game anyway?" asked Athena. "I wish I had. It's mega-fun!" Besides being the goddessgirl of inventions (just one of her many titles), she was also a good sport. Amid laughter, she went to sit in the "out" zone by Hestia, and the shell was soon thrown again.

Eventually the game narrowed to only two members on each team: Artemis and Calliope on Day, versus Aphrodite and Pheme on Night. But on the very next toss, which landed on black, Pheme managed to tag Calliope on the arm.

"I had an *idea* I might be the next one out," Calliope joked as she went to join the others on the fountain wall. Getting her play on words, several girls laughed. She hadn't been at MOA long, but long enough for everyone to know she was always full of ideas.

"Very a-*Muse*-ing," Amphitrite told her, grinning as she moved over to make room for Calliope to sit beside her.

Then the shell came up white, and only Artemis was left on the Day team to tackle both Aphrodite and Pheme from Night. All the girls sidelined at the fountain cheered on their remaining team members.

"Go, Artemis!" Calliope yelled.

Artemis raced after Pheme and Aphrodite, her

expression determined. As they passed the other girls at the fountain, Artemis's arm stretched out. Her hand *reeeached*. "Gotcha!" she crowed as she tagged Aphrodite on the shoulder. "At last!"

Laughing, Aphrodite collapsed onto the grass by the fountain. "Thank godness for that," she said, breathing hard. "I'm *pooped*. Plus, my makeup's got to be a mess by now. And I need new lip gloss and eyeliner. Guess I'll be going shopping at the Immortal Marketplace this weekend."

"Me too," said Artemis. The other girls looked at her in surprise. She hardly ever wore makeup *or* went shopping. "I don't mean the shopping part, but about being pooped," Artemis explained quickly. She looked over at Pheme. "Want to call it a tie?"

"Stop the game now, you mean? Okay," Pheme agreed readily. Then to Aphrodite she added helpfully, "I heard Cleo's Cosmetics is having a sale."

"Fizzy! I love that place," exclaimed Amphitrite, overhearing. "Maybe I'll go with you, Aphrodite. Cleo's has a waterproof line of makeup that really works."

Calliope supposed that waterproof makeup would be especially important to a sea nymph. Like Artemis, Calliope herself didn't bother with much makeup. Except for on special occasions.

Everyone sat together on the fountain wall now, talking about their weekend plans. A lot of them were going to the music festival in Athens tomorrow. Calliope was just thinking she needed to get back to her room to practice the new song, when Amphitrite spoke to her.

"Thanks again for your border idea in Architectureology today," said the mergirl. "I've decided to make one using crushed, colored shells."

"Sounds . . . fizzy!" said Calliope, and they both

grinned at her use of Amphitrite's favorite slang expression. "Your undersea garden is a cool idea. I hope it gets built."

Amphitrite slipped a comb from the pocket of her golden chiton and began to run it through her long turquoise hair. "It will."

"I like your confidence!" Calliope admired how positive Amphitrite seemed to be that Mr. Libon and Principal Zeus would pick her design as most creative and she'd get to see it built.

Amphitrite must have guessed what Calliope had been thinking. "Luckily for me, it doesn't matter whether Mr. Libon and Principal Zeus choose my design or not," the sea nymph told Calliope. "A committee of merpeople has already voted to build my garden around the Poseidon Palace, once construction on the palace is finished."

"Wow!" said Calliope. "That's fantastic! How great that you'll for sure get to see your design—"

Swoosh! She broke off as a sudden cold sprinkle of water showered all the girls.

Aghhh! Calliope and the others jumped up in surprise. It was the boys!

Apparently the Episkyros game had just ended. So Ares and Apollo had raced over, leading a bunch of the boys to where the girls were sitting. The boys had jumped into the fountain, splashing all the girls on the wall.

Typical godboy behavior, thought Calliope. They couldn't just come over and start chatting. They had to make an entrance that got them noticed! Amid screams and giggles, she had an idea. "Let's get even," she told the other girls. "How about a water war—girls against the boys?"

81

"Yeah!" the other girls shouted.

Soon everyone was splashing around in the pool at the base of the fountain, even Aphrodite. That girl was surprising. As the goddessgirl of love and beauty, she always appeared fashionable and "put together." Since she seemed to care a lot about looking her best, Calliope had pegged her as one of those girls who would shy away from messy activities like Ostrakinda or water wars. But Aphrodite was giving as good as she got.

At that very moment she was merrily slapping her hands against the water to create a wave that splashed her crush, Ares, right in the face. "Take that!" she shouted. When he splashed her back, she only laughed. She didn't seem to care that her golden hair was now wet and straggly and her chiton a soggy mess. Naturally, she looked every bit as beautiful wet as she did dry, however.

Calliope gave a squeal of surprise as a torrent of water suddenly cascaded over her head. Apollo, who was Artemis's twin brother, along with an apple-cheeked, golden-winged godboy named Eros, had ambushed her. Somehow they'd gotten hold of a couple of pitchers and were using them to good effect.

Before Calliope could retaliate, Artemis and Amphitrite leaped over to help her. Artemis put a finger to her lips and sent Calliope a significant look. Then she did a shallow dive into the fountain and swam toward Apollo. Seconds later he let out a yelp and fell backward with a splash. Calliope grinned, figuring Artemis must have grabbed his ankles and knocked him off balance.

Amphitrite's legs and chiton had turned into a golden-scaled tail as soon as she had hit the water, just like on swim night. Now, with a mighty flip of that tail, she sent a wall of water over Eros that doused him good and caused him to drop his pitcher. He flapped his wings to dry them, flinging drops of water everywhere.

Calliope grabbed Eros's pitcher as it bobbed closer. Quickly she scooped water into it and showered Poseidon before he could turn his water-spraying trident on her. Any one of those three *A* girls—Aphrodite, Artemis, or Amphitrite—would make a good roomie, she thought as she cheerfully battled on. She should ask one of them to spend the night with her so she could interview—um, *hang out* with them. But which one?

As usual, a great idea soon popped into her head. "Eenie meenie miney moe," she chanted under her breath while glancing in the direction of first one girl and then another. "Catch a Geryon by the toe."

She paused for a second. It had always been a mystery to her why anyone would want to catch a Geryon by the toe or by any other method. They were six-legged beasts with vicious talons, and they smelled like a combination of swamp gas, wet dog, and cow patties. But, whatever. That was just how the choosing rhyme went.

"If it hollers, make it pay—fifty drachmas every day," she continued. "My mother told me to pick the very best roomie for me, and you are SHE." When she reached the end of the rhyme, her glance landed on the goddessgirl of love and beauty. All righty! Aphrodite! Calliope would ask *her* to spend the nighty!

But as Calliope was making her way across the pool to talk to the goddessgirl, she glimpsed someone across the courtyard. Was that—*Homer*? It sure was!

Her heart began to beat fast. He was going up the granite steps to the Academy's big bronze doors. What was he doing here? Giddy to see him, she scrambled from the fountain. Then she raced across the courtyard and up the steps. She caught up to him just as he reached the top step. "Hi, Homer," she said breathlessly.

He smiled at her, but then immediately backed away. "You're dripping!" he exclaimed, holding his scrollbook bag away from her. "You'll get my stuff wet!"

"Hey, I'm not all that drippy," she assured him. "Just my hem." She bent, grabbed the bottom of her chiton, and wrung it out between both hands. It was wetter than she'd thought. Droplets spattered the granite under her feet. He moved another step away.

She automatically excused his fussiness. *He prob-*

ably has important scrolls in that bag. He worked hard
on his writing and wouldn't want bleeding ink to ruin it.
After all the time they had spent together, she knew
how careful and protective he was when it came to
his work.

Homer reached for the big golden door handles
and pulled open one of the Academy's front doors.

"A bunch of us were playing water wars," Calliope
told him quickly, desperate to hold on to his attention. "That's how I got wet."

"Uh-huh," he mumbled as she followed him
through the door.

"It was *sooo* much fun," she went on. "It was girls
versus the boys and—"

"Listen, Calliope," he said, interrupting her as they
stood in the entryway. "As much as I'd love to stay and
talk, I've got something I need to do right now."

"Research in MOA's library?" she guessed.

He shook his head. "Something else." He seemed a little jumpy about whatever it was, so maybe he'd come to see Principal Zeus with some request. As King of the Gods and Ruler of the Heavens, the big, loud, and powerful Zeus could be very intimidating. "Gotta run now," Homer said pointedly.

"Oh." Though disappointed to be shut out, Calliope tried not to show it. "Well, okay. See you later maybe? Like, tomorrow at the music festival at the Theatre of Dionysus? My sisters and I are singing in it, and our first number—"

"I'm not sure I'll be able to make it," Homer interrupted her again to say. Obviously impatient to be off, he'd been tapping one of his sandaled feet against the marble floor the whole time she'd been speaking. With a toss of his head, he added, "Later."

Then he strode off without waiting for a reply.

Calliope's stomach sank. Well, that had hurt. He had obviously been dying to ditch her. Sounded like he wasn't coming to the festival either. Would it have made any difference if she'd been able to finish telling him that the Muses' first song was going to be one he himself had written? She would have liked for him to come simply because he was interested in *her*, but hey, whatever it took! Too bad she hadn't had time to tell him about that first song.

Even in the entryway, she could hear the other students outside still having fun in the fountain. For half a second she considered rejoining them. She wasn't in the mood to go back down there right now, though. No, her wet chiton felt clammy against her skin. And her spirits were even damper. By chasing after Homer, she'd missed her chance to ask

Aphrodite to spend the night. She'd have to ask her the next time they saw each other.

Feeling deflated, Calliope went back to her room and changed into her comfiest, cutest pink pj's. They were decorated with musical notes and bits of lyrics she'd inspired musicians to write, and she usually wore them when her spirits needed a lift.

She climbed into bed with the music for the new song lyrics she needed to go over. However, the papyrus sheet soon slipped from her hand. It drifted to the floor as she fell asleep.

5

The Music Festival

Calliope wasn't usually nervous about singing in front of large groups. But the next morning she felt kind of shaky when she joined her eight sisters on the circular stage in the Theatre of Dionysus. The Muses were first up on the program. They all looked spiffy, dressed in the purple concert chitons they wore whenever they performed together. Her favorite big sis, Terpsichore, sent her a smile as they formed two rows onstage—four sisters in front, including Calliope, and five behind.

Calliope took a deep breath, trying to calm herself. The source of her nerves wasn't hard to figure out. She was not—no way, nohow—prepared.

She'd hoped to have time to go over the new song lyrics—the third of the song trio she and her sisters would be singing—a few times before the performance. But as luck would have it, she'd woken up late this morning. In her hurry to leave for the theater, she'd forgotten to bring the new song lyrics with her. And none of her sisters had brought lyrics either because . . . why would they? They'd already memorized them! Well, if necessary, she'd just have to fake it on the new song. Her sisters would cover for her.

Calliope glanced around the theater from her position second from the left in the front row. The building was a large open-air structure with a three-tiered stone seating area (now full of festival attendees) that stretched up the sloping hillside. The stage was downhill from the seats. The theater bore the godboy Dionysus's name because it had been built in his honor. He was MOA's best actor!

The Academy's pompous herald had been drafted as master of ceremonies for the festival. Soon he walked out to the front of the stage. *Ping! Ping! Ping!* As he struck his lyrebell, the audience quieted. "Good morning, mortals and immortals," he greeted them. "Welcome to this year's musical festival at the Theatre of Dionysus!"

He paused a moment, his eyes roving the crowd. Then, in a loud, important voice, he went on. "In case you have not yet heard, there has been a last-minute and very dramatic addition to this year's program—a new event that will take place directly after the first intermission. Yes, ladies and gentlemen, this morning you will witness the satyr Marsyas pitted against the godboy of music himself, Apollo! It will be the musical battle of the century!"

At this the crowd began to hoot and cheer.

The herald let this go on for a few seconds. Then he held up his hands, motioning for quiet again. "But before we get to that," he said after the crowd had calmed, "we have two phenomenal groups of singers here today for your listening pleasure."

He took a few steps to the side of the stage so that he was no longer directly in front of Calliope and her sisters. Then he made a grand sweep of his arm in their direction. "And so, without further ado, I give you a very special and melodious treat for your ears—the *nine Muses*!"

At a signal from Urania, Calliope and her sisters began their first number. It was Homer's "Hymn to Earth, the Mother of All." Since it was a song they performed often, Calliope relaxed into it and let her lilting soprano voice ring out.

> *"O universal mother, who dost keep*
> *From everlasting thy foundations deep,*
> *Eldest of things, Great Earth, I sing of thee!*
> *All shapes that have their dwelling in the sea,*
> *All things that fly, or on the ground divine*
> *Live, move, and there are nourished—these are*
> *thine . . ."*

She gazed out at the audience, some of whom were singing along. Aphrodite, Persephone, Artemis, and Amphitrite were all sitting together. They caught

Calliope's eye during the song and waved to her. She smiled at them, but of course she couldn't wave back. That would have been unprofessional!

When the song ended, the crowd erupted in applause. Calliope's heart soared at the warm response. If only Homer had been in the audience too, admiring her singing. And her sisters' singing as well, she mentally added quickly. But she liked to imagine him singling her out as special.

The Muses' second song was the chorus from *The Bacchae*, a tragedy by the playwright Euripides. It was a wistful, somewhat sad song that started like this: "Where is the home for me? O Cyprus, set in the sea . . ." When their song eventually came to an end, the crowd applauded with enthusiasm again.

Scanning the rows of seats nearest the stage, Calliope noticed several audience members quietly wiping tears from their cheeks. Then suddenly her breath caught. Was that *blue* hair she'd just glimpsed in the third row? *Spiky* blue hair? It was! She felt a thrill flutter in her chest. For there, smack-dab in the middle of the third row, sat the dreamy, talented, cute Homer!

Why hadn't she spotted him earlier? Maybe he'd arrived late? Who cared? At least he'd come! After his lukewarm response to her invitation yesterday, she really hadn't expected him.

When he happened to glance her way, she caught his eye and smiled at him. He gave her a curt nod, which, given Homer's personality, passed for friendly. Something about his standoffishness appealed to her, though. Because he was distant and hard to get to know, he seemed all the more intriguing.

Happily, she began singing the Muses' third song

on cue. It was during this number that she ran into trouble. Halfway through, she completely forgot her part! This was mostly due to a lack of practice, but also to an attack of nerves now that she knew Homer was watching.

She lapsed into silence and pretended to mouth the words. Since there were nine of them singing, she thought no one would notice, but when she had been looking at the song the night before, she'd neglected to note a solo part. *Her* part. Suddenly her sisters' voices dropped out.

Calliope froze in horror. For a measure or two there was dead silence. Then the sisters on either side of her, Melpomene and Erato, gave her a nudge. Calliope started in again, "Oh mighty Zeus doth bring great storms to vanquish the wicked and . . . um . . ." Having forgotten the rest of the line, she mumbled, "Something, something, something."

From somewhere in the audience came a surprised giggle. And whispers. Calliope's face went hot. Suddenly remembering the next line, she forged ahead. "So lift your voices in perfect harmony and sing like a beautiful bird!" Unfortunately, her upset from muffing the previous line caused her vocal cords to tighten up on the word "bird." The resulting note was way off-key and sour.

More uncertain titters came from the audience. Horrified, Calliope stopped singing altogether. Luckily, her sisters came back in to finish the final verse and chorus.

Don't look at Homer, don't look, don't, she told herself. But she peeked anyway, and saw that he was frowning at her. It figured that he'd finally pay attention to her at the one time when she'd rather he didn't! *Sigh.*

Despite Homer's obvious disapproval of her performance, relief washed over Calliope as the Muses left the stage. At least the disaster was over.

"What happened out there, Baby Sis?" Polyhymnia asked as they gathered offstage. Their other sisters leaned in close to hear Calliope's answer, wearing expressions ranging from irritation to concern.

"I . . . um . . . didn't memorize the lyrics well enough," she admitted.

"What? But you only had to learn one new song!" Euterpe said in a disbelieving tone.

"I know, I know. I'm so sorry," said Calliope. She avoided looking at Urania, who had, after all, offered to practice with her several times. Calliope hated letting others down, especially her sisters. And it was awful to think that, along with everyone else, Homer had witnessed her humiliation.

"Everything is still new at MOA. You must be very busy adjusting," Terpsichore said, sweetly coming to Calliope's defense.

"All those classes to study for," Thalia added understandingly.

"And anyway," Terpsichore went on, "I bet a lot of people in the audience didn't even notice anything was off."

Recalling her sour note and the titters that followed, Calliope doubted that, but just the same she was grateful to her favorite sister for trying to make light of the catastrophe. "Besides," Terpsichore added, "even if anyone did notice, they'll forget all about it as soon as the next group performs."

Calliope hoped she was right.

The sisters had just sat down in seats that had been saved for them in the second row, when the herald pinged his lyre again. "Next up, and without further ado, two numbers by a group called . . ." He broke off for a moment to pull a notescroll from his pocket. "The Nine Pie Rides!" he finished, sweeping his arm toward the group.

On cue nine princesses began walking downhill past Calliope and her sisters on their way to the stage. "That's Pierides—PEER-rih-deez," hissed a member of the new group.

"Yeah, is that so hard? Why does everyone say it wrong?" hissed another.

Calliope frowned. Yuck! The nine daughters of King Pierus of Macedon? She hadn't realized who the other group was going to be. But she and her sisters had run into these princesses at other performances. They were spoiled rich mortal girls who fancied themselves the Muses' equals. Their father encouraged their arrogance and had even given his daughters the same names as the nine Muses!

As they filed by, wearing diamond tiaras and chitons of the latest fashion, Calliope's Pieride counterpart glanced over at her. A snarky grin came over her face as she came to a brief halt. "Such an *aMUSEing* performance you gave in that last song of yours."

The Pieride named Urania gave a fake yawn, patting her mouth with her palm. "Not! It was a total Muse snooze!"

"Yeah, a real Muser-loser!" said the one named after Calliope's sister Thalia. Then all nine of the Pierides laughed scornfully and high-fived as they continued on down to the stage.

Wishing she could sink into the stone floor of the theater, Calliope stared down at her silver sandals, feeling utterly humiliated. Had Homer overheard those preening, presumptuous Pierides? Hopefully not. Though she'd been careful not to look directly at him when she'd sat down, she knew he was still sitting just several seats over in the row behind her.

"Those bratty mortals. How dare they!" muttered the true Urania.

"We can't let them get away with that, princesses or not!" muttered Euterpe.

"So what should we do?" asked Terpsichore as the Pierides began to sing their first number. It was called "Soar Like a Bird" and was a song the Muses knew well, since they'd often sung it themselves.

Rallying a little at her sisters' support, Calliope cocked her head and listened to their adversaries croon. At the same time, she was remembering her conversation about revenge with Medusa the night before. A sly smile came over her face. "I have an idea," she said.

After she shared her plan with her sisters, they all looked to Urania for approval, since she was the oldest. "Okay?" Calliope asked her.

"As a responsible adult, I can't approve this plan," Urania informed them. But then a mischievous sparkle lit her eyes. "Only, there was so much screeching onstage just now—hmm, or was that singing?—that I don't really think I heard the plan at all. I can hardly protest against something I know nothing about," she finished, giving them all a wide-eyed, innocent look.

Calliope grinned at her, knowing this meant they could put their plan into action. The Muse sisters waited until the Pierides were nearing the end of their song. Then, as those princesses sang the last line about "soaring over the heads of all," the Muses chanted a spell in unison:

"Girls into magpies. Take to the skies.

Chatter, chatter . . . scatter!"

At once, all nine Pierides morphed into black-and-white feathered magpies. Chattering in dismay, they rose into the air and did as magically instructed. They scattered. The audience broke out in applause and cheers as the birds swooped over them. Everyone probably figured the transformation was a planned part of the performance! (And in Calliope's opinion it was the best part, because no way were those pampered princesses better singers than her sisters.)

Instantly the herald took center stage again. "Now wasn't that a fun surprise! Thanks, Pie Rides!" he said quickly. "Guess they're off to their roost . . . er, home . . . in Macedon."

"That's PEER-rih-deez," one of the nine birds

cawed back before the magpies flew off toward the horizon.

"Looks like we'll be skipping over the Pierides' second number, however," the herald went on. "Instead we'll go straight to intermission. And when we return," he added, "it will be time for our special event. Marsyas versus Apollo in the musical challenge of the century!"

The audience cheered in anticipation.

"Do you think the Pierides will suspect that we're the ones who changed them into magpies?" Calliope asked her sisters.

Terpsichore grinned. "I hope so. Then maybe next time they'll pay us proper respect!"

Urania put her hands over both her ears. "La, la, la, *la*, la!" she sang out. "Good thing I didn't hear any of that!"

"If I hadn't flopped so badly, they wouldn't have been able to criticize us, though," Calliope said glumly.

Urania uncovered her ears and gave Calliope a quick hug. "Live and learn, Baby Sister. Next time you'll be better prepared, right?"

"Right," said Calliope, nodding like she meant it. Which she did. After all, if she wanted to be treated as a grown-up in her family, she really did need to be more responsible.

Terpsichore gave her a playful head noogie. "In my humble opinion, you need a bit of a break from MOA," she told Calliope. "I've got a dance recital tomorrow, but how about if the two of us meet in the Immortal Marketplace for some 'retail therapy.' Monday afternoon, say around four at the central atrium? We can shop till we drop and just have fun."

Cheering up, Calliope smiled. "I'd love that. Thanks!"

For the moment, all thoughts of her Architecture-ology project had flown away, just like the magpie princesses!

6
The Challenge

NOW THAT IT WAS INTERMISSION, A LOT OF people were leaving their seats to visit with friends in other parts of the theater. Homer might have still been in the row behind her, but for once Calliope didn't try to get his attention. He could be kind of a perfectionist, and she was too embarrassed about her musical mess-up.

She watched Aphrodite, Persephone, Artemis,

and Amphitrite rise from their seats a few rows away. They would probably be too polite to mention her botched performance if she went up to them.

"See you guys after the break," she said quickly to her sisters. "I'm going to go talk to some friends." If she could peel Aphrodite away from the others, maybe she could ask her to spend the night. Then, with luck, she might land a roomie! Would they share her room or Aphrodite's? she wondered excitedly.

But as she started up an aisle toward the girls, she heard Homer call out her name. "Calliope. Over here!" Unfortunately, he was set on a course to intercept her before she got to Aphrodite.

A picture formed in her mind, of his frowning expression following her muffed solo. Unable to face him so soon after her disastrous performance, Calliope pretended not to notice him. She felt certain that, unlike her goddessgirl friends, Homer wouldn't let politeness stifle his frank opinion of her singing snafu. Swerving in the opposite direction, she quickened her step.

Not daring to look back in case he was following her, she headed for a wooden building called the skene that was directly behind the stage. It was where scenery for plays was stored and where performers could make quick costume changes too. Hearing footsteps coming closer, she ducked inside.

Calliope pulled up short when she saw Apollo was sitting there in the small building. He was practicing scales on his seven-stringed lyre in preparation for his turn onstage. He stopped playing when he saw her. "So how did your performance go?" he asked.

She paused, one ear cocked toward the entrance. However, she relaxed when the footsteps she'd heard continued on past the skene, accompanied by voices, none of which was Homer's. *Phew.* Maybe he hadn't followed her after all!

Looking over at Apollo, she replied to his question with her own question, "You didn't hear us sing?"

He shook his head and plucked a couple of lyre strings. "I was practicing. Sorry I missed you guys, though."

"Don't be," Calliope said. Then she told him about forgetting the words to the Muses' last song, thus messing up her solo, and about her chagrin at the sour note she'd hit.

"Ouch," Apollo said sympathetically. "A singer's worst nightmare."

Calliope nodded. She peeked out the door and saw that the coast was clear. She wasn't taking any chances of running into Homer, though. "Okay if I stay a minute? Or are you . . ." She glanced at his lyre, wondering if he needed some alone time before he performed.

"No, it's okay. Might help to have company," said Apollo.

Huh? Was he hinting that he was nervous? Surely not. After all, he had performed gazillions of times. He even had a band called Heavens Above that played at MOA dances and other events.

Deciding to stay put a while longer, she started wandering around the room. As she idly studied various props, including a fake crown and a large plank painted to resemble a castle battlement, she spoke again. "My sisters were nice about my flub-up. But still, it was *humiliating*. And then those copycat Pierides princesses had to rub my face in my mistake. You should have heard their snarky remarks!"

It made her cringe to remember, but then she smiled. "My sisters and I got revenge, though. Ms. Nemesis would've been proud of us." MOA's Revenge-ology teacher was big on punishments when justice demanded them.

Apollo quirked an eyebrow, looking intrigued. "What did you do?"

Calliope told him about the magpie spell. "Since the song the Pierides were singing was about soaring birds, everyone in the audience thought the princesses' transformation at the end was a part of their performance," she finished up.

She was gratified when Apollo laughed so hard that he almost fell off his stool. "That's *classic*. Served them right," he said once he had finally managed to gain control of himself again. After a pause he spoke in a serious tone, almost as if to himself. "Seems like there are some who don't respect immortals anymore."

"I know! They hold us to an impossibly high standard," Calliope agreed, thinking of Homer now.

"Then, when we fail, they decide they're better than us and that it's okay to challenge us." Staring into space, Apollo frowned.

Although the two of them had been talking about the Pierides, Calliope guessed he was thinking about Marsyas and the musical battle that would begin as soon as the intermission was over. She picked up a couple of fake swords, studying them.

"*My word, how mortals take the gods to task!*" she said, brandishing one of the swords in a mock-fight as she began reciting her and Medusa's favorite quote from Homer's *The Odyssey*. "*All their afflictions come from us, we hear. And what of their own failings? Greed and folly double the suffering in the lot of man.*"

Apollo punched a fist into the air. "Exactly!" he crowed. "Homer sure got that right!"

"I wonder, though," Calliope mused, gazing at the shiny blade. "Maybe it's not a lack of respect that causes mortals and other Earth creatures to challenge the gods. Maybe the cause is their desire to be *like* us."

"Huh?" said Apollo. "You mean as in, they're jealous of us?" He'd idly begun to strum his lyre again.

"More like over-the-top admiration." Calliope pushed off a fake tree she'd begun to lean against. "Think about it." She wagged the fake sword at him as if it were her finger. "Mortals find immortals endlessly fascinating. We're like pop stars to them, the way they devour everything that's printed about us in *Teen Scrollazine*, and build temples to honor us."

"Hmm," said Apollo, still strumming. "You've got

a *point*." He glanced at the sharp tip of the fake sword she still held, and grinned.

"Ha-ha," Calliope said, getting the joke and grinning with him. She put the sword down and went over to peek outside once more. No one to the left, no one to the right. "Well, I guess I'd better go," she said. "Intermission must be almost over."

"Wish me luck?" Apollo called after her.

Surprised, she looked back over her shoulder at him. "Okay, good luck," she said. "But you won't need it."

"Maybe not," Apollo said, "but Marsyas really is an awesome musician."

So he *was* nervous! "Yeah, but you're the godboy of music," Calliope told him firmly. You can play that lyre upside down and backward! Don't worry."

Apollo grinned and hopped up, tucking his lyre

under one arm. "Thanks for the vote of confidence. Guess I'd better head out too. I'm up next."

With that, they both left the skene, separating as Apollo went down to the stage and Calliope went to rejoin her sisters in the audience. She kept an eye out for Homer along the way, but fortunately he was nowhere in sight.

She took her seat again as others in the crowd did the same. Down on the circular stage the herald, Marsyas, and Apollo were huddled together, discussing something. Finally they broke apart, seeming to reach some kind of decision.

The herald stepped to the center of the round stage and pinged his lyre to get the audience's attention. "Ladies and gentlemen. Mortals, immortals, and creatures," he called out. "Before we start today's mighty musical battle, our two fantabulous contestants will each choose three members of the audience. If you are selected, you will become part of a panel of six judges to determine the ultimate winner."

A murmur swept through the crowd. "What if there's a tie?" someone from the audience shouted out.

The herald puffed out his chest. "In the event of a tie, the contestants have asked *me* to cast the deciding vote." He was obviously proud that both Marsyas and Apollo trusted him to make that decision.

"What's the prize?" someone else called out.

"Winner gets a forfeit from the loser," Marsyas called back confidently. "Which means Apollo—uh, I mean, the *loser* has to fork over whatever the winner wants. No complaints."

At this, Apollo paled a little. *Why?* Calliope wondered. Deep in his immortal heart, he had to know he was a shoo-in for the win, right?

The herald took charge again. "Judges, when you are called, please come up to the side of the stage and be seated." He swept an arm toward six chairs that were now being set up.

Marsyas chose first. Hoofing it over to the herald's side, he patted his prized goat-hair vest, then smoothed it down with both hands as he surveyed the crowd for judges.

"Pick me! Pick me!" a few voices called out, until the herald gestured for quiet.

Marsyas made his first two choices immediately. "Echo and Daphne." With twin squeals the two nymphs jumped up from their seats and bounded down to the stage. They were best friends, and, more important, they were also Marsyas's friends. It was Echo, of course, who had designed Marsyas's vest.

"And Pan," Marsyas added, pointing at the top tier of seats. A fellow satyr who was also half-boy, half-goat, Pan was an excellent musician as well. He played the panpipes, an instrument of his own devising made from reeds. Bleating happily, Pan trotted down the nearest aisle to sit by the two nymphs onstage.

Then it was Apollo's turn to select judges. He stepped up to the herald's other side, opposite Marsyas. As he glanced out over the crowd, his gaze caught Calliope's. "I choose Calliope," he said with a smile. "And two of her sister Muses," he added. "She can decide which two."

Calliope's eyes widened in surprise. She would have predicted that he'd pick his crush, the princess Cassandra. And maybe his sister Artemis and his roommate Dionysus. She wondered if Apollo had only chosen her because he felt sorry for her after hearing about her doomed performance.

Regardless of the reason, this was a real honor! And she planned to take her job as a judge seriously— as befitted a responsible goddessgirl, one who was definitely no longer anyone's *baby* sister!

Her sisters were all looking at her, awaiting her decision. "I wish I could choose all of you," she said sincerely. "But since I can't, I pick Urania and Terpsichore."

Quickly she and her two sisters joined the other three judges at the side of the stage. Now the herald flipped a coin to decide which musician would play first. "Heads," Apollo called out, as Marsyas called "Tails" at the same time.

Apollo won the toss and walked across the stage floor to pick up his lyre, which was just a short distance away. The lyre was U-shaped, with a hollow turtle-shell body at the bottom curve of the U and a bar across the open top of the U. Its seven strings were of equal length but of varying thicknesses, and stretched from the crossbar at the top of the lyre to a fixed tailpiece. A smaller crossbar—called a bridge—was positioned on the turtle shell to lift the strings away. This would allow them to vibrate and produce sound.

A chair was brought out for Apollo, and he sat down. Before beginning to play, however, he took a few seconds to adjust the bronze tuning pegs along the top crossbar of his lyre, tightening or loosening the strings to change their pitch.

When all was ready, he began to pluck and strum a melody using the fingers of both hands, as one plays a harp. Notes rose and fell, at times fast and at times slow, always in perfect harmony. The audience listened, entranced. And when Apollo finished the tune, the theater broke into cheers and enthusiastic applause. Ares and Poseidon hooted the loudest. Calliope and her two sisters cheered right along with them.

Apollo, with his lyre in one hand and his chair in the other, moved to stand at the back of the stage. Then Marsyas clip-clopped to front and center, holding his double-reeded aulos. The pair of pipes were made of cane and had holes cut along their length. When he covered the holes with his fingers and blew through the mouthpieces, the pipes would produce different tones. Marsyas grinned at the audience and raised the instrument's twin mouthpieces to his lips.

Puffing out his cheeks and blowing mightily, he began to play a sprightly tune. His fingers zipped up and down over the holes. The rhythmical and penetrating sounds he produced were so exciting that they were practically as electric as the sparks that flew from Principal Zeus's fingertips!

Calliope traded looks of alarm with her sisters. She was sure that none of them wanted to decide the contest in favor of Marsyas, but it was beginning to seem like they might have no choice.

When Marsyas finished playing, the audience exploded in applause and cheers. Some even stomped their feet! The satyr grinned triumphantly at Apollo.

He knows he's won, Calliope thought.

But before she and the other five judges could officially vote on the winner, Marsyas, buoyed by the response of the crowd, couldn't resist pumping his fists in the air. "I am the greatest musician in the world!" he boasted. Turning toward Apollo, he added in a cocky voice loud enough for the audience to hear, "Tell you what. Because I'm so certain of my talent, I'm going to give you one more chance to beat me."

His eyes gleamed as he patted his good-luck goat-hair vest. "So what do you say, Apollo?" he asked with a wicked grin. "Want to give it another try?"

Apollo hesitated, looking uncertain. His gaze swept over the judges and then came to rest on Calliope. Seeing a glint of desperation in his eyes, she gave him an encouraging smile. Something seemed to come over him then. His look of desperation changed to one of hope, even confidence.

His shoulders straightened as he eyed Marsyas. "I accept your offer," he declared. "I just hope you won't regret having made it." He grinned a myste-rious grin and sent a meaningful glance at the vest. "Because," he explained, "I intend to nail your hairy hide to the wall."

Marsyas only laughed. "Whatever, god dude. But one more thing," he said, his eyes wild with glee. "If I win, I'll expect a lot for giving you this second chance. You'll have to leave Mount Olympus Academy and serve me in my woodland forest for the rest of my days."

The audience gasped. But Apollo just shrugged, surprisingly self-assured all of a sudden. "Fair enough."

Once again Apollo took center stage with his instrument. Standing to play, instead of sitting this time, he raised his lyre. Then he began to pluck and strum the very same lively song Marsyas had just played on his aulos. Only, Apollo played it twice as fast. And as if that weren't impressive enough, he suddenly flipped his lyre around so that the top crossbar was on the bottom. Holding the instrument over his head, he played the song *upside down*! Then he held the lyre behind his back and played it. And then he played it with his teeth. All without missing a single note.

When Apollo finished the song, he did air splits and threw his lyre into the crowd. His friend and roommate, Dionysus, caught it. "You rocked it, Apollo! I'll have this waiting for you when you want it back!" Dionysus called to him.

The amazed crowd roared their appreciation and approval. They applauded and stomped thunderously, and shouted "Bravo!"

Marsyas scowled, looking a little nervous for the first time.

Apollo glanced over at Calliope. Catching her eye, he mouthed the words, *Thanks, upside down and backward.*

Huh? Why was he thanking her, and in that odd way? She hadn't done anything to help him. *Hmm.* All at once she remembered what she'd said to him just before he'd gone onstage, about how he didn't need any luck because he could play his lyre *upside down and backward*. Her words must have inspired him to really try playing his lyre that way. Like most creative types, he'd taken her inspiration and built on it, until it had become something all his own. Something amazing!

The herald had taken center stage again. Apollo and Marsyas stood on either side of him as he looked over at Calliope and the other five judges. "So give us the verdict!" he called out to them. "When I place my hand over the head of each contestant, give a thumbs-up if you think he's the winner." He placed a hand above Apollo's head first.

Calliope, Urania, and Terpsichore thrust their thumbs into the air. Giving Marsyas apologetic looks, Pan, Echo, and Daphne did too.

"The decision is unanimous!" the herald announced to nobody's surprise. "Apollo wins!"

Shouts of approval rang out. "Woo-hoo!" "Awesome!" "That lyre was on fire!" After the audience's cheers finally died down, the herald asked Apollo, "What do you choose for your prize?"

Apollo grinned over at Marsyas. "Like I told you, I intend to nail your hairy hide to the wall, or at least just tack it there." He jerked his thumb toward the satyr's goat-hair vest. "Take it off, dude. That hide vest is going up on the wall of my dorm room as a trophy!"

Marsyas nodded sheepishly as the audience laughed and clapped. Then he shrugged off his hairy vest and handed it over to Apollo. "Take care of it. It's my pride and joy," he said.

"Don't worry," Apollo told him. "You can always grow another one."

"Yeah, in about ten years," grumped Marsyas. It sounded like he was hoping Apollo would take pity on him and let him keep the vest. But Calliope doubted that Marsyas would've done that for Apollo, and she didn't feel too sorry for him. He'd brought this on himself by challenging Apollo to a contest in the first place. And not being satisfied with humiliating Apollo once, Marsyas had tried to do it a second time. Not smart. Not smart at all.

Though more groups were scheduled to play or sing after a second intermission and the festival would go on till afternoon, Calliope and her sisters had stuff to do. After giving up their seats to new arrivals, they headed out of the theater.

"Calliope!" She turned to see that Homer had caught up to her at last. "Can I talk to you?" he asked.

Though still embarrassed about her flawed performance, she returned his smile with a bright one of her own. "Sure," she said.

"Alone?" he added, sounding a little uncertain.

Whoa! He had something private to tell her? A little thrill of happy anticipation zipped through her. Maybe he wasn't going to lecture her after all. Maybe he was going to ask her to go to the Supernatural Market to sip nectar shakes or something like that. She stepped a few feet away from her sisters to talk with him.

Just then she noticed that he was holding a bag in one hand and cradling a notescroll in his other hand. She eyed the scroll. What was written on it? Could it be an ode to a sweetheart? Was he going to give it to *her*? *Thump-thump* went her heart.

"Here," Homer told her. But instead of handing her the scroll, he handed her the bag.

"Can you put this in the Hero-ology classroom?" he asked. "I found it under my seat in the theater. I tried to give it to you earlier during the intermission to take to MOA. I don't want to entrust it to just anyone."

Calliope gave him a quizzical look as she took the bag.

"I imagine Mr. Cyclops will be glad to have what's in it back," Homer said. "I think they're the game pieces from the Hero-ology game board. I heard they were missing, and I remembered them from when I visited his classroom."

"What?" Calliope said in surprise. She peered into the bag, which was indeed full of three-inch heroes, and then she looked back at him. "These were stolen! Hero-ology classes have had to use shells to play the map game ever since they went missing. How weird that the thief left them *here*!" She glanced around in bemusement.

"Yeah, it's a mystery," Homer said lightly. "I wonder if Principal Zeus or Mr. Cyclops have any suspects in mind." After a slight pause he added, "Not that it matters, since the pieces are back now, I guess."

Quickly he changed the subject, nodding in the direction of the empty stage, where she and her sisters had sung. "Amazing performance up there earlier, right? Despite a few glitches."

"Amazing? Really?" So he didn't think she'd messed up that badly? If he'd thought she had, he'd have said so. Or was this his way of trying to be sweet? She smiled at him. And glanced at the notescroll still in his hand.

She was disappointed when he tucked the notescroll under his arm. There probably wasn't an ode written on it after all, she realized. Just research notes for whatever piece of writing he was doing now.

"Speaking of glitches," he said with a frown. "What happened to you up there?"

"Huh? I thought you just said my performance was amazing," she replied.

"No, I meant *Apollo's* playing was amazing. The second time around, anyway. Marsyas made a huge mistake, letting him play again."

"Oh," said Calliope. "That's true, but I was hoping you were going to say . . ." She broke off, waiting for him to offer her some kind words of consolation about her botched performance. Really, though, she should have known better than to hope for such a thing.

"You know, you really should have practiced more," he informed her.

Duh! Obviously she knew *that*! And, anyway, if she hadn't spent so much time helping him with his *Iliad* and *Odyssey*, she probably could've learned a zillion songs by now. Did he ever think about *that*? No, that was an unfair thought, she decided. Her part in inspiring both of those scrollbooks had happened long before she'd needed to learn the song she'd mangled today.

She was so stung by his unfeeling manner, however, that she started to hand him back his bag. How dare he ask her for a favor and then insult her like this. But she didn't return the bag. Because that might've meant a delay in getting the game pieces back where they belonged.

Just then Urania called to her, gesturing toward some chariots parked nearby. "Hurry up, Calliope. We need to get going." Accompanied by a half dozen festival-going students from MOA, she and her sister had traveled to the theater in one of those blue and gold Academy chariots.

Calliope turned back to Homer, who was already walking away from her. He wasn't even going to say bye?

Hurt, she blurted, "Well, gotta run, Homer, but thanks for the oh-so-helpful advice. I mean, it was totally inspiring for me," she said, unable to keep a snarky note from her voice. Not that it mattered. Her sarcasm was lost on him anyway.

"You're welcome," he said over his shoulder. *For Zeus's sake.* He really did think she was grateful for his criticism! "And be careful with that." He glanced meaningfully at the bag she held.

Before she could reply, a pretty, ponytailed mortal girl approached him clutching a scroll in her hand. It turned out to be a copy of *The Odyssey.*

Calliope tarried a moment longer, watching her speak to Homer, who suddenly wasn't in such a hurry to leave. She looked about his same age, three years older than Calliope.

Sounding starstruck, the girl gazed admiringly at Homer and gushed, "I can't believe it's really you! I love *The Odyssey*. I've read it three times!" She thrust her scrollbook at him. "Will you sign my copy?"

"Sure," said Homer. He took a feather pen from the pocket of his tunic and expertly unrolled the scrollbook to a blank space before the actual beginning of his epic poem. Pen poised, he asked, "What would you like me to write?"

The girl batted her ridiculously long eyelashes at him. "How about 'To Chloe, with all my love'?"

Godsamighty! thought Calliope. She was going to barf. She waited for Homer to tell this crazy girl he'd write no such thing.

But instead he only laughed while flushing to the

roots of his spiky blue hair. "Um . . . sure," he said, sounding flattered.

"Calliope!" Urania called again. "C'mon. Hurry up."

Reluctant to leave before the ponytail girl did, Calliope waved at Urania and slowly started toward her sister. But she kept her head turned over one shoulder, her eyes glued to the drama unfolding between her crush and that dumb girl.

Chloe batted her eyelashes some more. "Your prose is, like, *sooo* inspired," she cooed.

Calliope paused midstep, waiting for Homer to credit *Calliope* for inspiring the prose. When he did, she was going back over there to wedge herself between those two. Urania could wait.

But all Homer said was, "Yes, writing epic poetry isn't easy. You wouldn't believe how hard I worked on that scrollbook."

"Ooh! I would, though," said the girl. "It shows."

Grr! In a total snit now, Calliope whipped her head forward and stomped off for the chariot. Homer's bag bumped against her leg the whole way there. Couldn't that dweeby crush of hers have acknowledged her help even a little bit? She was totally done with him. *Forever.*

"Everything okay?" asked Urania, looking past her toward Homer.

No, everything was not okay. Her feelings were hurt. "Mm-hm. Fine," said Calliope.

But seconds later, as the chariot she had boarded sailed over the theater, she couldn't keep herself from glancing back at Homer. When he looked up to smile and wave at Calliope, her newly frozen heart suddenly melted all over again. Maybe he was just being polite to a fan. After all, that girl had been quite pushy about getting her scrollbook signed.

He'd probably just been flustered by that "love" thing she'd asked him to write and hadn't been thinking when he'd replied to her question about how hard it had been to write *The Odyssey*. And it *was* true that he'd worked hard on it. He *should* be proud of his work. She'd inspired it, but he'd written it. So him taking credit was fair. *That's just the way creative people are,* she told herself. And just like that her wilted crush on him blossomed anew.

But he was still talking to Chloe when the chariot rose above the clouds and Calliope could no longer see them. Would he invite the girl to the Supernatural Marketplace? At the thought, a dull ache settled in Calliope's stomach.

7

Tidying Up

ONCE BACK AT MOA, CALLIOPE RAN DOWN THE hall to the Hero-ology classroom. She reached out to twist the doorknob, then hurried across the room and dropped the bag Homer had given her on top of Mr. Cyclops's desk. The teacher would be sure to discover it first thing Monday morning.

Then she slipped out of the room and carefully closed the door behind her. Check that errand off her to-do list, she thought as she hurried upstairs to her room to change out of her purple concert chiton. She was happy to have helped both Homer and Mr. Cyclops. Not to mention all the students who needed to use those figures in class. Good-bye, shells! She'd be kind of sorry to see them go, because students had decorated them in funny ways with ink and string and other doodads to give them the character of the heroes they'd replaced.

Emboldened by her success at returning the Hero-ology figures, she decided to invite Aphrodite straightaway to sleep over that night. So after she slipped out of her purple chiton and into her favorite turquoise one, she went down the hall to Aphrodite's room and knocked.

"At music festival. Be back late. I'd love it if you leave a message," said Aphrodite's voice. It seemed to be coming from the pink feather quill pen, which was attached to the heart-shaped wipe-off notescroll hanging on her door.

Calliope sighed. Quickly she took the pen from its holder, intending to write on the heart-shaped scroll. But then she stopped. She'd really rather deliver her invitation in person, not write it where everyone who walked by could read it. She set the pen back in its holder.

Maybe she should have stayed at the festival longer too. She'd kind of wanted to get away before anyone else brought up her big mistake, though. Plus her sisters had been leaving, and she had schoolwork to do. As it turned out, she'd had Homer's bag to deliver as well. Probably most of the MOA students who had gone to the theater that morning were still there— the ones not behind on their homework, anyway.

Unable to face the loneliness of her dorm room, she decided to do homework in the MOA library instead. Quickly she gathered up some supplies—her plan-scroll, list of ideas, pens, and so forth—and headed downstairs. Unfortunately, the library proved no easier a place to study than her room. Distracted by a multitude of scrollbooks on every imaginable subject, she pulled out one after another and got even more project ideas. As if she needed more. Not!

She was reading about gymnasiums and considering what it might be like to design one with multiple indoor tracks and a covered chariot racetrack too, when Principal Zeus entered the library. His arms were full of old scrollazines, which he proceeded to dump on a table four over from hers.

Mr. Eratosthenes, the librarian, hurried out of his office at the side of the library. "Can I help you?" he asked softly, coming over to Zeus. The librarian was the quietest person Calliope had ever known. Pretty much the complete opposite of the principal!

"Hera says I need to tidy up my office," Zeus announced in his booming voice. "So I brought you my old copies of *Temple Digest* and *Great Principals Quarterly*."

"Splendid," Mr. Eratosthenes enthused in his quiet voice. He rubbed his hands together, seeming truly delighted to have them.

Zeus grinned. "Don't suppose you've got a use for other stuff from my office too? Hera has decided I need new chair cushions, even though my old ones are perfectly good. They've got a few scorch marks on them is all. She even wants to replace the artwork on my walls." He scratched his head, adding, "I thought the painting I made of Pegasus was genius, but she

147

says otherwise. You've seen it. What do you think?"

"Um." Mr. Eratosthenes paled and looked uncomfortable.

Calliope had a feeling he was trying to think of something tactful to say so as not to hurt Zeus's feelings. (Homer could take lessons from him in that department!)

She had seen that Pegasus painting when she'd first come to MOA and been called to Principal Zeus's office to meet him. The so-called work of art hung on the wall in a prominent spot, directly behind his enormous desk. You couldn't avoid seeing it when you were talking to him.

There was a printed title next to it that read, *Pegasus in Flight*. Rumor had it that Zeus had added that so there'd be no doubt about the painting's subject. Good thing too, because she'd never have guessed it was supposed to be a golden-winged flying horse. Zeus was terrific at a lot of things, but art wasn't one of them. She'd never tell him so, but his Pegasus piece looked like it had been finger-painted by a five-year-old!

"I'll gladly take the scrollazines," Mr. Eratosthenes told Zeus in a voice Calliope had to strain to hear. "But unfortunately, the library doesn't collect chair cushions and artwork."

"Right, I knew that. Just thought I'd ask," Zeus said, nodding. "I'll find some other place to donate them. And if I can't, I may just have to keep them!" He grinned craftily, looking like he kind of hoped that would happen.

After the principal left, Mr. Eratosthenes gathered up the scrollazines. Seconds later Artemis, with her bow and quiver of arrows slung across her back, came in. "Hi, Mr. Eratosthenes," she said with a little wave. "I'm here to pick up a scrollbook I put on hold."

He peered over the top of the scrollazines piled up in his arms. "One moment," he said quietly. "I was just going to put these in my office to process later. Afterward I'll get your scrollbook for you."

"Okay. Thanks," said Artemis. She perched, half-sitting on a table to wait, and whipped out a little pumice stone. After pulling an arrow from her quiver, she began to use the stone to sharpen its point.

Now was the perfect chance to get to know her a little better, thought Calliope just in case Aphrodite didn't work out as a roomie as she'd previously hoped. Catching Artemis's eye, she smiled. "Hi. I'm Calliope, remember?"

"Of course, I do," said Artemis. "You were on my Ostrakinda team last night. So, what's up?"

"Just doing homework for my Architecture-ology class," Calliope went on. That was stretching the truth, since she'd spent most of her time so far dipping in and out of various scrollbooks and jumping from one idea to another, but whatever.

"I have Architecture-ology first period," Artemis responded, moving closer to Calliope's table so they could talk more easily.

"Really?" Here was something they had in common, then. Besides liking to play Ostrakinda, that was. "What's your project?" Calliope asked.

Artemis pulled out a chair and plunked down opposite her at the table. "An archery range," she said, an excited look in her eye. "I actually finished early and turned in my planscroll yesterday. I'm just here to pick up a book to read for fun."

"Lucky you," said Calliope. She made a face. "I

haven't even decided for sure what my project will be yet."

"Whoa," Artemis said, her eyes skimming the pile of scrolls that lay on the table between them. "That's leaving things late. I wouldn't want to be in your sandals right now." She cocked her head. "You're a Muse, though. You must have a ton of ideas."

Calliope shrugged. "Ideas are easy. It's choosing just one and developing it into something really great that's the hard part."

Artemis grinned. "So it's hard for a Muse to be her own muse?"

Calliope laughed. "You got it. That's *exactly* my problem." Glancing down at the scrollbooks scattered all over the tabletop, she added, "I thought coming here to work would help, but it just widened my choices. Not what I needed. Don't you just love libraries, though? I could *live* in one!"

"Hey," said Artemis. "Maybe you should design a library, then. For your project, I mean. If you choose something you're interested in, it makes the work easier, don't you think? That's why I asked if I could design a new archery range. I have lots of ideas for improvements to try." She broke off as Mr. Eratosthenes returned with her library scrollbook.

Calliope considered Artemis's suggestion as the goddessgirl stood to take it from him.

"Due in three weeks, please," the librarian announced softly.

"Thanks," said Artemis. As she took the scrollbook, Calliope glimpsed the title—*Arrow Aerodynamics.* Not the kind of scrollbook *she* would read for fun, but it figured that Artemis would. She and her twin brother, Apollo, were MOA's champion archers.

"Well, good luck with your project," Artemis said to Calliope as Mr. Eratosthenes went back to his office. "I'm off to my room." Hugging her scrollbook, she started to leave the library.

"Wait!" After quickly gathering her stuff together, Calliope raced after the goddessgirl. "I really like your project suggestion," she told Artemis, falling into step beside her. "A library design might be just the thing." As they climbed the stairs to the dorm, she said, "I don't suppose you'd want to hang out in my room so we could talk some more?" She hoped she didn't sound *too* desperate for company.

"Sure, why not?" Artemis said. "Oh, wait. I've got archery practice in a few minutes. I was only going up to drop off my scrollbook before leaving again."

"Oh, well, some other time, then," Calliope said, trying not to sound as disappointed and loser-ish as she felt.

They reached the fourth-floor landing and pushed through the door to the girls' dorm. "Tell you what," Artemis said as they started inside, "why don't you come by my room after dinner tonight instead? We can hang out."

Calliope nearly jumped for joy. "Sure!" Since *her* room was just inside the dorm hall door, she quickly bid Artemis, "Bye till later."

Once inside her room, Calliope began to sing a happy tune as she dropped her supplies onto her desk. Maybe, just maybe, she and Artemis would really hit it off, and the two of them would wind up rooming together. Wouldn't that be just perfect?

Not only that. Thanks to her chance meeting with the goddessgirl of hunting and archery, her Architecture-ology project might soon be back *on target*!

8

Square One

BY DINNERTIME MOST OF THE MOA STUDENTS
who had gone to the music festival had returned.
Luckily, when they saw Calliope in the cafeteria, no
one said a word to her about her major flub during
the Muses' performance. Was it possible they'd all
forgotten about it? She hoped so.

She had seen Artemis in the cafeteria, and they'd
waved before sitting down with friends at different

tables. When Calliope got back to the dorm, she went down the hall to Artemis's room and knocked on the door. Immediately she heard barking.

"Come in!" Artemis called out.

The very second Calliope opened the door, Artemis's three dogs leaped upon her and began to lick her all over.

"Off!" Artemis scolded her hounds as she tried to make them behave. After another minute of doggy greeting, they obeyed. Glancing back at Calliope, Artemis introduced her pets. Pointing first at her bloodhound, then the greyhound, and lastly at the beagle, she said, "Suez, Nectar, and Amby."

"I forgot you had dogs," Calliope said. Which was silly of her, since Artemis's three hounds were a common enough sight around the school. Somehow she just hadn't thought about the fact that they lived in her room. So in a way, this goddessgirl already had roommates—three drooly ones.

Artemis motioned for Calliope to take a seat on one of the beds, so Calliope did. She liked dogs, but rooming with them and a roommate in tight quarters would certainly be a . . . challenge. "Where do they sleep?" she asked as Artemis plopped down on the edge of the other bed.

Artemis dipped her head toward the bed Calliope was now sitting on. "There," she said just as Nectar leaped up beside Calliope. He turned around in circles before finally curling up against her leg. Settling his head in her lap, he stared up at her.

Aww, how cute! thought Calliope as she reached to scratch him behind the ears. Cuddling up with a dog or two might be nice, right? But would they all fit? Artemis's dogs were big. Nectar alone took up almost half the bed. If she wanted a roomie, she couldn't afford to be *too* picky, though.

"So, about your Architecture-ology project . . . ," Artemis prompted after a few seconds.

"Yeah, well, I liked your suggestion of a library. And I'm thinking I'd design the outside of it to look like a temple but outfit the inside with shelves for scrollbooks," Calliope told her.

"Cool," Artemis said. "Mortals go to temples to show their respect for the gods, so by designing your library to look like a temple, you're encouraging respect for knowledge!"

"I am?" Calliope said in surprise. She'd only picked a temple design because temples were big and could hold a lot of scrollbooks! But then again, it was certainly possible that the idea of respecting knowledge had been in her mind all along. Her experience as a Muse had taught her that it wasn't unusual for writers and artists to miss seeing themes in their own work that others easily uncovered. Sometimes it was hard to see what was right in front of you.

Apparently bored by the subject of schoolwork, Nectar jumped down from the bed. His nails clicked across the floor as he headed for the water bowl beside Artemis's desk. As he lapped up some water, Artemis looked at Calliope. "I know we just ate, but how about a snack?" When Calliope seconded that idea, Artemis brought out some chips and dip.

Calliope borrowed a few sheets of papyrus and, while munching on chips, made a sketch of the outside of her library-temple building. All along the front she drew Ionic columns. They seemed a good fit for a library, since their tops were scroll-shaped. Artemis looked on, making suggestions along the way.

"Ye gods," Calliope exclaimed after a while. "I just noticed I'm getting crumbs all over the place."

Artemis glanced up from the arrow tip she'd begun to file. "Who cares?" she said with a shrug. "Just brush them onto the floor. My guys will eat 'em."

It was nice to know the goddessgirl wasn't a clean freak, thought Calliope, doing as Artemis had suggested. She wasn't exactly neat herself, though she was a *bit* neater than Artemis. Compared to other girls her age, she was probably *medium* neat. Not super-tidy, but not super-messy, either.

The second the crumbs hit the floor, the dogs ran over and scarfed them down. Then Suez leaped onto the bed to search for more. Unfortunately, when the big dog landed, he knocked the container of dip off the bed, along with Calliope's sketch. The dip splattered everywhere, but Artemis never batted an eyelid as her dogs just licked up the mess.

When Calliope picked up her sketch from the floor, she saw there was now a smear of dip in the middle of it, as well as a tear. *Oh well,* she thought as she wiped the sketch off. Maybe Mr. Libon would be so happy to have her turn something in on Wednesday that he wouldn't care about a little smudge or tear.

Good thing I'm easygoing, Calliope thought. She could put up with Artemis's dogs if Artemis was interested in rooming together. Eventually she opened her mouth to suggest a tryout sleepover, but just then the girls heard shouts in the hallway.

"Sounds like trouble!" Artemis said. Looking fierce, she grabbed her bow and arrow and leaped for the door.

Calliope jumped up from the bed to follow. Artemis opened her door, but before either of them could step into the hallway, the dogs rushed out ahead of them. Just then a flat ring-shaped rainbow about ten inches in diameter shot from the far end of the hall. The thin ring glided right over the top of a surprised Nectar's head and settled around his neck like a loose collar.

There were hoots of laughter from girls clustered together at the far end of the hall as the greyhound shook his head from side to side to get rid of the rainbow collar. Once it slipped off, Nectar and the other two dogs chased after it as it flew back down the hall, leaving a long trail of sparkly rainbow dust in its wake. It landed in the hands of a pink-haired goddessgirl named Iris. She was the goddess of rainbows and could make them in whatever size or shape she wanted.

"Come play with us!" Athena called to Artemis

and Calliope. "Iris thought up this cool game. The object is to toss this magical rainbow ring onto a doorknob along the hall. The farther the doorknob, the more points you score for ringing it."

"But you get zero points if you miss," said a brown-haired girl named Antheia. She reached up to straighten a cute wreath of ferns and berries that encircled the top of her head like a crown. She was the goddessgirl of flowering wreaths and also Iris's roommate and BFF.

Artemis tossed her bow and arrow back into her room. After whistling for her dogs and temporarily shutting them in her room again, she and Calliope headed for the group at the end of the hall. Amphitrite smiled at the two of them as they came over. She must've been the one who'd thrown that last ring, because now she cocked her head at Iris and asked, "That wasn't *exactly* a miss, was it? After all, I did ring *something*."

The girls all giggled again. Then Aphrodite spoke up from the group. "Not only that. It was a moving target besides!"

"Moving targets are harder to aim for than stationary ones," commented Artemis.

She would know, thought Calliope. Artemis must've had plenty of practice aiming at both in archery matches. Although it seemed clear that Amphitrite had ringed Nectar by accident, it had still been an amazing feat.

"Twenty points, then," Iris announced cheerfully. "Who wants to go next?"

"Me?" asked Pandora reaching for the rainbow ring. Even when something wasn't a question, Pandora made it sound like one. Her blue-and-gold bangs

165

were a mark of her super-curious nature, often taking the shape of question marks.

Iris handed Pandora the rainbow ring. Right away the curious girl accidentally flung it straight up in the air. "Oops," said Pandora as the ring hit the ceiling directly above the group of girls. It ricocheted off, then plummeted down to land squarely (or rather, *circlel-y*) around the dozen snakes atop Medusa's head, looking like a colorful crown.

"Sorry!" said Pandora. "I guess my aim isn't very good?"

"Ya think?" Medusa remarked wryly.

But there was no real harm done. Since the rainbow ring was made of actual rays of colored light, it weighed nothing at all. Medusa's snakes wriggled out from under it in no time, and the ring flew back to Iris.

Artemis went next. Using her archer's eye, she took careful aim before flinging the rainbow circlet. It shot down the hall all the way to Calliope's door and neatly ringed her doorknob.

"Bull's-eye!" Calliope congratulated her as everyone cheered. This wasn't *exactly* the same thing as an arrow hitting the center of the target, but it seemed close enough, and Artemis seemed to understand what she'd meant.

"Score! That's worth fifty points and puts Artemis is the lead," Iris announced.

Several more girls took turns. Two of them scored zero and two ringed doorknobs halfway down the hall, for twenty points each.

Finally Calliope volunteered to try her luck. As she drew the ring back, preparing to fling it, it slipped from her hand and plopped to the floor behind her.

"Ye gods, I flubbed that one!" she exclaimed in dismay. But then she glanced over at Iris and grinned. "Do you give negative points?"

The girls all laughed. "That one doesn't count," Iris said generously. "Try again."

So she did. This time she managed to ring a doorknob that was three quarters of the way down the hall. "Woo-hoo!" Calliope shouted when Iris awarded her a respectable thirty points. This was fun! She felt like one of the group, fitting in with everyone and laughing and hanging out. It was the same kind of feeling she'd had growing up with her sisters back home.

After three rounds the game finally broke up. Since hurling rainbows with great accuracy was second nature to Iris, she had taken herself out of the competition. Therefore, to nobody's surprise, Artemis was declared the winner. Her potential roommate truly was quite an athlete, Calliope thought admiringly. She herself had placed somewhere in the middle of the group's scores, which was totally cool with her.

When the two girls returned to Artemis's room, her dogs slunk away with their tails tucked, instead of running to the door to greet them. "Uh-oh," said Artemis. "They only act like that if they're expecting to be scolded. What did you do, guys?" Both girls glanced around the room.

Then Calliope gasped, spotting the now empty bowls for the chips and dip. They licked those bowls clean. And my design! Oh no!" Not only had the dogs polished off the snacks, but they'd also chewed her library design for Architecture-ology class to shreds.

"I'm *sooo* sorry!" Artemis exclaimed. "It's probably because your paper had dip on it. It smelled like food." Meanwhile, her dogs guiltily avoided looking either girl in the eye, as if they realized that Artemis had been apologizing on their behalf.

"It's okay," Calliope said lightly. "I can make a new sketch tomorrow."

Sensing that she wasn't too mad, the dogs began to tentatively wag their tails. And when she knelt on the floor at their level and smiled at them, they went wild with relief. They leaped upon her and licked her hands and face. She patted Suez's head, rubbed Nectar behind his ears, and scratched Amby's stomach. "Yeah, I forgive you," she murmured to them.

Although these guys were sweeties, she could clearly see now that rooming with three rambunctious dogs would be a greater challenge than she was up for. Even if Artemis had been willing to consider becoming roommates, Calliope wasn't going to ask. *Nope. Sharing a room with Artemis—and her dogs—was out.*

Which meant she was back to square one on the roommate search. Plus, she'd have to redraw her design. Still, thanks to Artemis, she at least had an idea for a project now. She wished she felt wildly excited about it, but already her original enthusiasm had dimmed. Maybe that was okay. A library was a more practical idea than a cloud-based chariot-racing arena, for sure!

After petting each of the dogs one last time, she said "Night" to Artemis and went up the hall to her lonely room.

9

A Fresh Look

ON MONDAY MORNING THE ACADEMY WAS
abuzz with the news of the mysterious return of the
Hero-ology classroom game pieces. Apparently Mr.
Cyclops had found them on his desk first thing when
he'd come in before the start of classes. Though
Calliope was bursting to tell someone the part she'd
played in the figures' reappearance, she held back.
She'd begun to wonder if there was something more

to Homer's story about finding the game pieces, and if he might actually know the real thief's identity. Who could he be covering for? Someone at MOA? A student? A teacher?

When she entered Architecture-ology class at the end of the day, she went straight up to Mr. Libon at his desk. "I've decided to design a library for my project," she told him.

"Excellent," he said. "Glad to hear you have a direction now." She cringed when he added, "Especially since the project is due in two more days."

"I have a rough sketch," she said quickly. She'd redrawn it on Sunday. As she took it from her schoolbag and handed it to him, she told him how Artemis's dogs had chewed up her first sketch.

He laughed. "So you're saying that a dog ate your homework? For real?"

She smiled. "Uh-huh."

"Well, thanks for this," Mr. Libon said. "I'll look it over. You can have it back at the end of the period."

"Okay. Thanks," said Calliope. Just then the lyre-bell chimed, so she went to take her seat.

When Mr. Libon stood up to address the class, a few random building model parts tumbled from his desktop to the floor, but he paid no attention to them as he began to speak. "Over the weekend I had a chance to think more about the project ideas you've all been working on and discussing. They're all generally good as far as they go. . . ." He paused to look around the room. "But many don't go far enough."

The class seemed to heave a collective sigh, and they all looked around at each other in surprise and concern. *What did he mean by that?* Calliope wondered anxiously.

Mr. Libon leaned forward. "While it's fine to repeat elements of a building design already in existence, I want you to strive to add something new or different. As an example, think about how Doric columns evolved into Ionic columns and then Corinthian columns. They went from simple to complex, right? Each change added something fresh."

Uh-oh, thought Calliope. Could she honestly say there was anything particularly *fresh* about her library design so far? Not really. Yes, she'd made her library look like a temple, but lots of buildings resembled temples. And the shelves inside her temple were just what you'd expect to see in any old library.

"To get a fresh look at something, sometimes two or more heads are better than one," Mr. Libon went on.

"Then Ms. Hydra must be really good at taking a fresh look at stuff, since she's got *nine* heads," joked Poseidon.

Mr. Libon gave him a tolerant smile as numerous students laughed. Then the teacher had the students count off to randomly form five groups of four or five students each. "Within your group you are to take turns asking questions about each other's designs in order to generate ideas to help make those designs more distinctive," he instructed them. "Get creative. Set your minds free. Think, 'What if . . . ?'"

Yeah, like *what if* Mr. Libon hadn't decided to make this project even more complex, thought Calliope. It turned out she was a number three, so she moved her chair to the back of the room to work with her team. Poseidon, Amphitrite, and Dionysus were also threes.

In typical fashion Calliope was able to come up

with all sorts of good ideas for the others in her group. They spent a lot of time talking about Amphitrite's undersea garden, the theater Dionysus was designing, and Poseidon's plan for a new water park. But the end-of-class lyrebell rang before Calliope could even share her library design.

"I'm so sorry we used up all the time," Amphitrite told her. "It wasn't fair that you didn't get any feedback on your project. Though, you probably don't need anyone's help, being a Muse. I bet you've got more great ideas than you can even use."

More ideas than she could use? Amphitrite didn't seem to realize that having lots of ideas wasn't necessarily a good thing. Thank godness Artemis had suggested an idea that Calliope felt she could run with. Even if it wasn't a fresh idea like Mr. Libon wanted.

"S'okay," said Calliope as the four threes grabbed

their chairs to move them back to their desks.

"No, it's not," Amphitrite insisted, dragging her chair alongside Calliope's.

Suddenly it occurred to Calliope that she was passing up a golden opportunity to check out Amphitrite as possible roommate material—to see how they got along when it was just the two of them.

"Well, it *would* be nice to discuss what I'm working on with someone," she said. "I mean, if you aren't busy tonight, maybe we could get together after dinner?"

The girls reached their desks and shoved their chairs under them. "Oh, sorry," said Amphitrite. "I'm busy tonight. Poseidon's giving me a tour of some of his water parks. I'm hoping to get ideas from him for building myself a fountain here at MOA, where I can sleep at night." She paused. "But I have time to talk about your project now if—"

Calliope interrupted her with a shake of her head. "I'm meeting one of my sisters at the IM this afternoon to go shopping." So much for choosing this girl as a roommate candidate. Calliope was not up for sharing a fountain! Amphitrite could breathe underwater, but Calliope definitely could not.

"Sounds fun," Amphitrite said brightly. "I still feel bad that we didn't get to talk about your—"

"You ready?" Poseidon called to her from the doorway just then.

"Oh, sorry, gotta go," Amphitrite said to Calliope quickly. "We'll talk more tomorrow, okay?" With that, she grabbed her pearl-beaded schoolbag and took off.

Calliope stopped by Mr. Libon's desk on her way out of class to pick up her library design sketch. "It's a start," he said with a small smile as he handed it back.

"Yeah, I know I still have a lot of work to do," she replied as she slipped the sketch into her bag. She probably should remain at school to work on her project in her dorm room instead of going off to the Immortal Marketplace, she thought as she left Architecture-ology and went by her locker to stash her bag. Still, she was really looking forward to spending time with Terpsichore. And a girl couldn't be expected to do homework *all* the time! She'd get a "fresh" start on work later tonight.

At the entrance to the Academy, she shucked off her regular sandals and grabbed a pair of winged ones from the communal basket inside the doors. Outside, at the top of the granite steps that led down to the marble courtyard below, she slipped the sandals onto her feet. Immediately their straps twined around her ankles and the silver wings at her heels began to flap. In a burst of speed she skimmed down the steps and across the courtyard, moving mere inches above the ground.

The wind whistled in her ears as she whipped down Mount Olympus to the Immortal Marketplace, which had been built beneath the cloud line halfway between the heavens and Earth. Within minutes she was skidding to a stop at the IM's entrance. After loosening the straps around her ankles, she looped them to hold the silver wings in place, allowing her to walk at a normal speed.

The IM was a lavish indoor mall topped by a beautiful high-ceilinged crystal roof. Rows and rows of columns separated the marketplace shops, which sold everything from the newest Greek fashions to tridents and thunderbolts.

When Calliope reached the central atrium, she

spied her sister right away. Dressed in a filmy pink dance chiton and dance slippers—her preferred attire even when she wasn't performing at a recital—Terpsichore was pirouetting around the atrium fountain. She squealed with joy when she saw Calliope, and danced over to give her a hug.

"So how did yesterday's recital go?" Calliope asked as they left the atrium to begin their shopping.

"Fine," Terpsichore said. Grinning, she added, "I didn't trip and fall, anyway."

"Ha!" Calliope said. Terpsichore *never* tripped or fell during performances. Her dancing was always flawless and won high praise from reviewers for the *Greekly Weekly News* and other news-scrolls.

"Let's stop here at Cleo's," Terpsichore said when they came to the makeup shop. "I could use a new lip gloss."

"Good idea. Pheme said Cleo's is having a sale," Calliope informed her.

The purple-haired, three-eyed owner of Cleo's Cosmetics wasn't around when they went in. So they walked up to a sculpted bust of a beautiful goddess that sat on the glass-topped counter. The head statue was surrounded by tubes of lip gloss and bottles and boxes of eye powders and liner, creams, and blushes.

"May I help you?" the head asked in a rather snooty voice.

Terpsichore pointed to a tube of pale pink lip gloss. "I'd like that one, please."

"Certainly," the statue replied. "Anything else?"

An idea popped into Calliope's brain. "Yes, please. My sister and I would like you to do our makeup," she announced.

Terpsichore stared at her in surprise. Then a

knowing twinkle came into her eye. "Hoping to impress someone?"

No wonder her sister was surprised. Calliope had never shown much interest in makeup. "Yeah, I'm hoping to impress upon my sisters that I've grown up," she replied cheekily. In other words, makeup might help her look more like the grown-up goddess-girl she was trying to be, and less like a baby sister!

"Mm-hm," said Terpsichore. It was a half-amused, half-suspicious sound.

What was her older sister thinking? Calliope had only made her makeover suggestion on the spur of the moment. As both girls took seats on cushioned stools at the counter, numerous boxes and bottles in front of them popped open on their own. A half dozen makeup brushes of varying sizes jumped from one of the boxes. Three flew to Calliope, and the other three to Terpsichore. The brushes hovered in the air before each girl for long seconds, as if considering what shades and techniques to try on them.

Then Calliope's brushes abruptly swooped to dip themselves in the various containers of makeup on the counter. One flew back to her and began to dust sparkly gold powder onto her eyelids, while another dusted pale powder over her nose. Its bristles tickled a little, and Calliope sneezed.

"Sorry!" she said when the brush reared back in alarm.

Terpsichore laughed. "So . . . from what I saw at the music festival, you seem to have made several new friends at MOA," she said as a makeup brush swished blue powder onto her eyelids.

"Yeah, the girls are pretty cool," Calliope said as

another of the brushes swept a pinky-red blusher across her cheeks. She knew Terpsichore was proud of her for getting accepted at the Academy, so Calliope didn't admit that she missed her sisters horribly and was longing for a roommate.

"And how are your classes?" Terpsichore prodded.

"I'm designing a library for my Architecture-ology project," she blurted. She hadn't meant to bring that up. The words had slipped out only because it was worrying her. "A special library for serious scholars," she added, having just decided on this. "With scroll-books about all the newest discoveries in science, history, and the arts."

"Oh, kind of like the Museum in Alexandria, Egypt?" Terpsichore said.

Calliope blinked. "Yes, kind of like that," she conceded. She hadn't really been thinking about that place, but her idea was kind of similar. Too similar? Her heart sank.

Terspchore laughed. "Remember how the guys who built it told us it would make a perfect home for us Muses? And that's why they named their library a *muse*um?"

Calliope remembered and shot her sister a smile. An orangey-red lip gloss that had flown over and begun to dash color onto her lips patiently backed away as she spoke. "Yeah. As if we would have wanted to grow up anywhere besides the springs and meadows of beautiful Mount Helicon. I mean, we already had a home!"

"Please!" the snooty head on the counter commanded. "Let the artists do their work!" The sisters grinned at each other but remained still and silent for the final minutes of their makeovers.

Before leaving Cleo's, Terpsichore insisted on buying Calliope all the makeup she'd tried on, which included the orangey-red lip gloss. It really looked great with her red hair.

Just outside the shop the sisters ran into Aphrodite. She was holding two large shopping bags that appeared to be full of new clothes.

"Love your makeup!" she exclaimed to Calliope.

"Thanks," Calliope said, pleased. After all, Aphrodite knew what she was talking about when it came to fashion and makeup. As the goddessgirl of love and beauty, she must also know a lot about crushes. Which would be useful knowledge for a roommate to have. Quickly Calliope introduced Aphrodite to her sister, then asked, "Need some help with those bags?"

Aphrodite's blue eyes sparkled as the three of

them began walking down the mall, side by side. "No need. My bag-carrying muscles are in good shape. Lots of practice. Shopping's my passion, what can I say?"

"Where do you keep so many clothes?" wondered Terpsichore.

"Good question! I've already filled both closets in my room and one in Artemis's room too," admitted Aphrodite. "Pretty soon I may need to take out my spare desk and put in some drawers or another closet!" She laughed, which made her look even more beautiful, if that were possible.

Hmm, thought Calliope. It didn't sound like there was any space left for another person in Aphrodite's room. Not a person with clothes anyway. And Calliope did own some clothes, though not nearly as many as this girl. She wondered if she should cross

Aphrodite off her list of potential roommates. But she liked her. Hey! Maybe Aphrodite could turn her entire room into a closet and come live in Calliope's room. There was a "fresh" idea!

Calliope was thinking about bringing up the subject of roommates, when Aphrodite said, "It's great that Artemis lets me use her spare closet. Except for the dog hairs that sometimes get on the chitons I store in her room, that is.

"I have a kitten named Adonis that I share with my friend Persephone," she told Terpsichore. "He sheds some too, but brushing him usually keeps things from getting too hairy in my room. Messes drive me crazy. I'm a real neatnik."

Walking on either side of her, Calliope and Terpsichore exchanged glances and then broke out in grins.

"What?" asked Aphrodite, looking from one to the other of them.

"Since there are nine of us Muses, we shared rooms at home," Terpsichore told her. "All of us were a little messy in our own ways, I guess. My dance shoes and stuff were always lying around."

"It wasn't like we were slobs, but none of us were exactly neatniks, either," Calliope added.

"Understandable," Aphrodite said cheerfully. When they paused at a shop window, Terpsichore began doing stretches. She could never stand still for long.

I wouldn't like having to keep things as clean as a café kitchen, Calliope thought as Terpsichore bent to touch her toes. But it kind of seemed like that was what Aphrodite might expect of a roommate. Sighing, Calliope mentally crossed Aphrodite off her possible roommate list. The way things were going, she might have to start thinking about getting a pet herself, because her roommate prospects weren't looking so good. But Zeus had to approve any pets brought to MOA. Since she was fairly new at the Academy, why would he do her any special favors? She wouldn't dare to even ask!

"Ooh! Look at that!" said Aphrodite. She pointed to a white chiton with overlays of pink silk on display in the window just beyond the one she'd stopped at.

"Wow! It's amazing," said Terpsichore. "And it would look great on you."

Suddenly Aphrodite dropped one of her bags. Cupping her fingers behind one ear as if to better hear something, she leaned closer to the store window where the chiton was showcased. "What's that? I think it's calling my name," she told Calliope and Terpsichore. Straightening, she laughed again, grabbed the bag she'd set down, and took a step toward the shop door. "Guess I'd better say bye, unless you guys want to come in and shop too?"

Just then Terpsichore's stomach grumbled. She put a hand over it and sent them an embarrassed grin. "Maybe I'd better get something to eat."

With giggles and waves Terpsichore and Calliope bid Aphrodite farewell and made their way to the Oracle-O Bakery and Scrollbooks shop. It was right across from the atrium and next to a twenty-foot-tall carousel with a platform wide enough to accommodate three rows of fantastical animal rides. MOA students had built the carousel and created the creatures upon it before Calliope had started school at the Academy.

"Mmm. Perfect snack stop. You in?" Terpsichore asked.

"Sure," said Calliope. "I'm kind of hungry too."

Cassandra, who was Apollo's crush and a Trojan princess, was behind the glass counter of the bakery when they walked in the door. Or rather, when Calliope walked in. Her sister *danced* in.

"Ooh. Your shop's gotten bigger!" Terpsichore exclaimed to Cassandra as she twirled up to the counter.

"Yes," Cassandra said with a smile that lit up her almond-shaped eyes. "My family thought our customers might enjoy more choices. So now we sell a variety of other desserts besides cookies. And we also thought our customers might like something to read while they snack. So Oracle-O Bakery and Scrollbooks is now two shops in one. Bakery in here. Scrollbooks for sale in there." She gestured toward an open archway that connected through to the new half of the shop, where shelves of scrollbooks stood.

"Nice idea. Snacks and reading go great together," Terpsichore approved.

Cassandra picked up an empty bag bearing the store logo and leaned slightly forward over the counter. "Now, what can I get for you two?"

Terpsichore made up her mind quickly. "I'll have that cupcake," she said, pointing at a pink frosted one with red sprinkles. "On a plate, thanks."

"Coming right up!" Cassandra got it for her, and then looked expectantly at Calliope. "And for you?" she asked as Terpsichore took a bite of her cupcake and moaned at its deliciousness.

"I don't know. I can't decide," Calliope said with a frown. She was practically drooling as she took in the large assortment of layer cakes, cupcakes, and pies that were now on display in the glass cases, in addition to all kinds of cookies. But just like with her

Architecture-ology project, having more choices to consider only made it harder for her to choose!

Eventually she settled on a bag of chocolate chip Oracle-Os, her all-time favorite cookie. The ones they served in MOA's cafeteria spoke your fortune aloud as soon as you bit into them, but the ones in the shop had written fortunes inside.

With their sweets in hand, the two girls wandered through the archway to the scrollbooks side of the shop. Calliope did a double take and nearly dropped her bag of cookies when she saw Homer there, sitting at a table. He didn't notice them at first since he was busily autographing a scrollbook for a boy— one of his fans, apparently. A sign on the wall behind Homer read AUTHOR SIGNING TODAY.

"Hey, there's Homer!" Terpsichore said, nudging Calliope. "You know him, right? Didn't you guys hang out while he was writing *The Odyssey*? And I saw you talking to him at the music festival Saturday."

Typical, thought Calliope. One sister or another was always in her business. But she didn't mind so much when it was Terpsichore.

"So what's he like, anyway?" her sister asked after taking another bite of her cupcake.

Having forgotten how miffed she'd been at him on Saturday when he'd failed to credit her for inspiring him, Calliope replied dreamily, "Awesome."

"As in crush-worthy?" teased Terpsichore.

Calliope could feel her cheeks redden.

A slow smile spread over Terpsichore's face. "Aha! I knew there was another reason for your sudden interest in this stuff." She held up the little bag of makeup they'd purchased and jiggled it teasingly. "I'm right, Baby Sis, aren't I?"

"Ha!" Calliope said, her blush deepening. When it appeared that Homer was finishing up with his fan, she darted over behind one of the scrollbook shelves, dragging Terpsichore with her. That way, Homer wouldn't see *them*, but they could see *him*.

As Calliope peered out at Homer between the shelves, Terpsichore finished off her cupcake and then grinned. "You *do* like him. I can tell," she said. Gracefully she bent her knees outward to each side in a plié.

"Shh," Calliope whispered.

"Why don't you go offer him a cookie?" Terpsichore suggested.

Calliope rolled her eyes. "Yeah, maybe I can replace the fortune inside it with one saying: *You should crush on Calliope.*"

They both giggled. "Go!" Terpsichore urged. She

gave Calliope a gentle shove toward Homer as the fan left his table. "I'll slip over and chat with Cassandra while you talk to him."

"Okay." As soon as Terpsichore left, Calliope sidled up to the table.

"Calliope!" Homer exclaimed. He beamed at her. "Thanks for coming to my signing."

He seemed so happy to see her that she decided not to admit that she hadn't actually known about the signing and had only happened on it by accident.

"Want a cookie?" she asked instead. She opened her bag and held a cookie out to him. When a crumb fell onto one of the scrollbooks, his expression changed to one of alarm.

He jumped to his feet and hastily brushed the crumb away. Then he got down so that his eye was level with the tabletop to check for any additional stray crumbs.

Satisfied that he hadn't missed any, he straightened to glower at her. "No, I do not want a cookie. And please keep them away from my scrollbooks!"

Godness! Calliope took a step back. Why did he always have to be such a . . . noodge!

Just then another boy fan came up to Homer with a copy of *The Odyssey*. He looked at Calliope, then stepped past her when he saw she wasn't holding a scrollbook to be signed. "Autograph it to me, please," he said to Homer. "Name's Lemnos." The boy leaned in closer. "I heard you're giving away free action figures with every scrollbook?"

"Um . . . yeah," said Homer. He signed the scrollbook quickly. Then, after shooting Calliope a furtive glance, he reached down to a box on the floor beside his chair. From out of the box he drew a small three-inch-high action figure.

Calliope saw at once that the figure greatly resembled the Hero-ology game piece of Odysseus.

"Wow, cool!" said the boy as Homer handed him the figure. Immediately he pushed a button at the back of the toy. Odysseus's arms, which had been balled into fists at his sides, popped up as if to punch out an enemy. Engrossed in pushing the button over and over, the boy started to walk away.

"Hey, don't you want the scrollbook too?" Homer called after him, sounding a bit peeved.

"Oh yeah," said the boy, turning back. Still playing with the toy Odysseus, he slipped the scrollbook under one arm without even looking at it. "Thanks," he said.

"Action figures?" Calliope said to Homer once the boy had left the shop. Homer smiled a little nervously. Her brain was working a mile a minute. It wasn't long before she put two and two together.

"It was *you* who stole the Hero-ology game pieces from Mr. Cyclops's room!" she accused. "You didn't just find them at the theater."

"Shh! I didn't steal them," insisted Homer, looking around in alarm to make sure no fans were nearby to overhear. "These action figures are based on some loose sketches I made of the game pieces when I hung out in the Hero-ology room a while back. It was when I was writing *The Odyssey*. Just ask Apollo or Aphrodite or anybody about that. It's true."

"Your action figures are too perfect to have been created from loose sketches," Calliope insisted, picking one out of the box and examining it.

Homer huffed out an exasperated breath and then leaned forward to take the piece from her, speaking quietly. "Okay, okay, but keep your voice down." He let out another long sigh, then admitted, "You're right, I'm the one who *borrowed* the game pieces. But you should be thanking me. I did it for *our* book—yours and mine—to help boost sales. I only meant to keep them for a day or two, while my publisher commissioned an artist to draw likenesses of the game pieces that were better than my sketches."

"So you could use those likenesses as models for your toy giveaway?"

He nodded. "Unfortunately, the artist took forever. But when he finally returned the game pieces on Friday, I tried to put them back where they belong. Remember how I showed up at the Academy when you guys were playing around in that fountain? Only when I went to the Hero-ology classroom, Mr. Cyclops was in there working late on lesson plans, which meant I couldn't sneak the hero figures back onto the game board, so . . ."

"So instead you lied and tricked me into returning them for you by giving them to me at the festival the next day," Calliope finished. *Our* book, indeed. He'd never referred to *The Odyssey* as *their* book before! He was just trying to get on her good side now so she wouldn't rat him out about this.

Homer nodded sheepishly. "You understand, right? And you won't tell Mr. Cyclops or Zeus? They were both really rooting for *The Odyssey* to do well. Sales did start strong, but I kind of panicked when they went into a little slump due to a competing book by another poet." He frowned as he said this, but the frown turned into a grin as he confided excitedly, "These action figures have shot sales of my scrollbook sky-high again!"

So now it was *his* scrollbook once more? Typical. What hurt most, though, was that he hadn't trusted her enough to be straight with her from the start.

"You do know that those game pieces control the movements of the actual mortal heroes they represent," she said.

He shrugged. "That's only true if the game pieces are physically on the game board at MOA. Take them off, and they don't affect the real heroes anymore."

"Still, if anything devastating had happened to those pieces while in your possession . . . Well, it just doesn't bear thinking about!"

"Mmm-hmm. Could you move a little?" asked Homer.

Huh? Calliope looked behind her to see that another fan was approaching with a copy of *The Odyssey*. While Homer signed it, Calliope glanced through the store's archway to see Terpsichore staring at them, a grin on her face. She obviously thought things were going well in here. Ha!

Once the fan left with his signed scrollbook and an action figure of Agamemnon (king of Mycenae and supreme commander of the Greek troops during the Trojan War), Homer turned back to Calliope. "So, have you been practicing your singing?" he asked. It seemed an obvious attempt to shift the topic away from one that was uncomfortable for him—namely game pieces and action figures!

"No, I haven't really had time," she replied testily.

Homer tsk-tsked. "How do you expect to do better during your next performance if you don't make time to practice?"

"I'm surprised you don't call it *our* performance when I sing. You do like to take credit for things I also have a hand in."

He looked genuinely startled. "What are you talking about?"

At this, Calliope exploded. "I'm talking about how I've had it with your lectures and your selfishness!" she exclaimed. "You say I was your inspiration, but you never . . ." She broke off, unable to continue for a moment. Finally, choking back a sob, she snapped, "You only care about your writing and yourself! Period."

Homer stared at her in shocked confusion. "No way! Of course you're my inspiration," he assured her. "The only reason I give you suggestions to improve yourself is because you're also my *friend*." He frowned. "Right?"

Calliope glared at him. "Right." Knowing what Homer was like, she guessed she shouldn't have been surprised at his willingness to go to any lengths— even stealing the precious Hero-ology game pieces— to further his author ambitions. And she'd been fooling herself to think that he'd ever see her as more than just a friend. Though in her opinion, he didn't really know how to be a friend back. Unfortunately for her, his scrollbooks were probably the only thing he would ever crush on!

To her dismay, as she was thinking this, a teenage girl came toward them with a tray of cookies. She looked about the same age as Homer and was very pretty, with long black hair and dark blue eyes. Oh yeah, it was Cassandra's sister. Calliope had seen her around the bakery before.

"Hey, Laodice." Homer smiled at the girl in a way he'd never smiled at Calliope.

"Hey, Homer," Laodice responded. Then she giggled as if they'd just shared some private joke. "Want a cookie?" she asked, holding out her tray.

"Sure," said Homer.

Calliope's eyes almost bugged out of her head

when, instead of freaking out because he feared getting crumbs on his precious scrollbooks, Homer took a cookie from Laodice. No, not just *one* cookie, but a whole *handful* of them! "Thanks," he told her. "Your cookies are the best!"

Staring from one to the other, Calliope suddenly realized that they were crushing! On each other. She guessed she should have known that if Homer ever did fall in like, he'd probably choose a girl his own age. Someone such as Laodice. Feeling a bit sick at heart, Calliope excused herself and hurried away. Not that Homer noticed.

Terpsichore met her as she came through the archway into the bakery half of the shop and headed for the door. "Ready to go?" her sister asked, following her.

Calliope nodded, forcing herself to smile.

As they stepped outside the shop, she saw Aphrodite

and Ares hanging out with Artemis and Actaeon across the way in the atrium. They were all waiting in line for tickets to ride on the IM carousel.

Calliope's gaze flicked to the awesome scenes painted atop the carousel's peaked roof. There was mighty Zeus bringing down a Titan with one of his thunderbolts, and Athena dressed for battle, wearing a pointy helmet and clutching a spear and shield. Carved around the roof's edge were colorful flowers, rainbows, and cute kittens that looked an awful lot like Adonis.

When the carousel started to load, Calliope couldn't help noticing the sweet way Ares was smiling at Aphrodite as they held hands and approached the platform. A pang of longing went through her. Homer had never tried to hold her hand.

All the carousel animals were taller than their riders and had been painted and polished till they gleamed. Calliope watched Actaeon give Artemis a boost onto the back of a white, golden-horned deer. Artemis had probably made that particular ride, since it looked like the deer that led her chariot.

Actaeon climbed onto a spotted leopard, a stately stander on the other side of Artemis's jumper. Stately standers—the rides that didn't go up and down on their poles—stood closest to the carousel's center. Jumpers—the rides that could pump up and down on their poles—stood along the outer edge.

Artemis and Actaeon laughed together as the carousel began to go around. They waved to Aphrodite and Ares, who were riding side by side on a white swan and an owl.

Calliope sighed. Maybe someday she'd experience that kind of liking too, she thought. Just not with Homer.

Terpsichore nudged her and nodded toward the carousel. "Want to ride it?"

"Sure, why not?" said Calliope. The carousel had picked up speed and become a whirl of jewels, mirrors, and colors. Homer would probably never agree to ride a carousel, she thought as her big sis bought the tickets. He'd think it was a silly thing to do, or a waste of time, and say he had writing to do if she asked him. But if Laodice asked . . . Calliope sighed again, knowing his answer to *her* might be different.

When the carousel slowed to a stop, Calliope waved to Artemis and Aphrodite and their crushes as they climbed down from their mounts and exited into the atrium. Then, choosing a jumper, she climbed onto the back of a lion, and her sister boarded a sheep right behind her.

As the carousel turned and their mounts went up

and down on their poles, Calliope's spirits lifted. She gazed at the shops whizzing by. Each one held a different collection of goods, from scrollbooks to clothing to weapons and more. Yet all the shops were housed inside one marketplace. In her mind this spinning vision of the IM somehow blurred and slowly fused with her current ideas for her Architecture-ology project.

Suddenly a whole new idea for her project popped into her head. Like many of her best inspirations for others, it had come from blending two separate ideas together.

A giddy excitement filled her. Because, wonder of wonders, for once she had inspired *herself*. And she knew in her heart of hearts that this inspiration was both fresh and doable!

10

More Inspiration

BACK IN HER DORM ROOM THAT NIGHT, CALLIOPE
excitedly jotted notes about the big idea she'd gotten
while spinning around on the carousel, so that
she wouldn't accidentally forget anything before
morning.

As she changed into her pink, musical-note pj's,
she caught sight of the painting of Homer on her
wall. She waited for a wave of sadness to wash over

her, knowing they'd never be an "item" like Artemis and Actaeon or Aphrodite and Ares, or any of the other crush-friendships at MOA.

The sadness did come, but it was softened by the certainty that dumping him was absolutely the right thing to do. Well, maybe "dumping" wasn't exactly the best word to describe what she'd done. She wasn't sure if you could actually dump someone if you'd never had a romantic relationship with them in the first place. But whatever.

Homer was talented, famous, eccentric, and intriguing. But he wasn't fun unless you were helping him work. So maybe she'd never really been as into him as she'd thought. Maybe it was only the *idea* of having a crush that she'd liked. After all, as a Muse, she was all about ideas!

"Farewell, my crush," she told the Homer painting.

Then she took it down and retired it to the bottom drawer of her desk. Hopping into bed, she snuggled under her covers, thinking of her project. The only crush on her mind right now was whether Mr. Libon or the other students in class would *crush* her new idea once they heard it. She hoped not!

When the lyrebell pinged to signal the start of Architecture-ology class the next day, Mr. Libon stood up from his desk and made an announcement. "I've become aware that not all of you had time to get brainstorming help on your projects yesterday," he said, twirling his compass on two fingers.

While he was saying this, Amphitrite grinned at Calliope from a few chairs away, raising her eyebrows up and down. *I told him. To be fair,* the girl mouthed silently.

Calliope smiled back. *That was awfully nice of her,* she thought. In a way, Amphitrite reminded her of her sister Terpsichore. Both were thoughtful, sweet, and kind. Thinking about some of Amphitrite's undersea garden ideas, Calliope added "clever" to the two girls' similarities.

"Therefore, please divide into the same groups as yesterday to continue sharing," Mr. Libon finished. "I'll come around and check in with each group."

As she picked up her chair and moved to where her group was meeting at the back of the room, Calliope was suddenly glad she hadn't had a chance to share on Monday. Because now she'd be able to share the *new* project idea she'd thought of. But as excited as she was to do so, she was also nervous. What if it wasn't as good as she thought? There would be no time to come up with anything else. It was now or never.

217

"All right," said Poseidon once he, Dionysus, Amphitrite, and Calliope were all seated together. "I think Calliope's the only one of us who didn't get to share. Want to go ahead?" He nodded at her.

"Sure. Thanks," Calliope said. Gazing around at the faces in her group, she asked, "So, have you heard about the Museum in Alexandria?"

Poseidon and Dionysus gave her puzzled looks. However, Amphitrite nodded. "I've read about it. Wasn't it named after you and your sisters?"

"Huh?" said Dionysus. Then his violet eyes lit up. "Oh! I get it. MUSE-ee-um."

"Yeah, but what is it?" asked Poseidon.

"One of those libraries where you go to look at scrollbooks," Amphitrite supplied.

"Then why isn't it just called a library?" asked Poseidon.

"I don't know," Calliope said, a little exasperated. She just wanted to get on with telling them about her new project idea! Still, after a moment's thought, she said, "Maybe 'museum' makes it seem special? After all, it's not just a place to store really old and important scrollbooks. It's also a place to read them, think about them, and talk about them with other thinkers. It's the most popular library—or *museum*, I mean— for scholars who want to do important research."

Amphitrite cocked her head at Calliope. "So what's this got to do with your project?"

Calliope took a deep breath. "Well . . . my idea for a project is to create a museum that's more than just a collection of scrollbooks. Think of it like the IM, which has lots of fascinating shops, each with a different kind of collection of things to sell. So my museum would have a bunch of rooms instead of shops, each with a different collection of things to study."

"Collection of what?" asked Dionysus.

"You name it," said Calliope. Getting excited, she shaped her idea in the air using both hands, inviting them to "see" what she envisioned. "Picture a room for jewelry, and another room for artwork, and another room for pottery."

"I bet scholars and philosophers would love to do research in a place like that," Amphitrite said to her. "Is that who would use your museum?"

Calliope stared at her, stumped. "Well, I . . ." She halted, unsure what to say. The question of who her museum was for was something she hadn't really considered yet. So far, she'd mostly been focused on the museum's design. Amphitrite's question was a good one, however—one that Mr. Libon had asked everyone to answer in their project write-ups.

Suddenly Calliope remembered something she'd said to Apollo before his contest with Marsyas last Saturday. Namely, that mortals and other Earth creatures were fascinated by the gods. "We're like pop stars to them," she'd told him. And just like that, a new inspiration sparked in her brain.

"My museum would be for everyday mortals!" she declared. "It would be chock-full of artifacts such as jewelry, artwork, and pottery like I said, but those would all relate to the gods." Then she added something that she knew would capture Poseidon's and Dionysus's interest. "There could even be a room with a collection of weapons."

"Cool!" the boys chorused.

"But where in Zeus's name would you get all the artifacts?" Dionysus asked her.

At once a new idea zinged into Calliope's head.

"Zeus! That's it!" She snapped her fingers. "I'd get them from donations. The other day I saw Zeus donating his old *Temple Digest* and *Great Principals Quarterly* scrollazines to MOA's library. But he had other stuff he wanted to donate that wasn't appropriate for the library. Like some scorched cushions, and you know that Pegasus painting behind his desk?"

"*Pegasus in Flight*?" Poseidon said, his turquoise eyes going wide. "I can't believe he'd get rid of that. He painted it himself. It's classic Zeus."

"Yeah, so be sure to put it in the very back of your museum," Dionysus suggested in a deadpan voice. Everyone cracked up. They'd all seen the painting and knew Zeus was no judge of art. No artist, either.

Calliope explained further. "While I was in the library, Zeus told Mr. Eratosthenes that Hera had convinced him to clean out his office. She was the one who suggested that he get new chair cushions and replace the artwork on his walls."

"Mortals would be awed by those old cushions if they could see them," said Amphitrite. "The scorch marks are powerful evidence of Zeus's might."

As if he'd forgotten that Calliope's museum wasn't real but just a project design, Poseidon piped up with an offer. "If you want, I could donate a couple of tridents from when I was little for your weapons collection."

"That would be fantastic!" Calliope enthused. She pulled a notescroll and feather pen from her schoolbag and made a note of Poseidon's suggestion. Everyone in her group—herself included—was talking as if her museum were actually going to be built.

Only a few days ago she would have been happy just to pass Architecture-ology with a decent grade, but now she found herself wishing for more. Wouldn't it be great if Principal Zeus and Mr. Libon decided on her museum as the most creative and interesting project design? Then her museum *could* become a reality, just like Amphitrite's undersea garden.

"How about a musical instruments room?" Dionysus said suddenly, drawing her attention back to the present. "I've got an aulos you could have."

"And how about a seashell collection?" Amphitrite added. "My sisters and I have tons of them, mostly cute or rare specimens."

Calliope was so busy jotting down their ideas that she didn't notice that Mr. Libon had been standing behind them, listening in. He looked intrigued. A good sign.

"Great work, Calliope!" he said with a smile. "Keep going." Then he moved on to another group.

Her heart leaped with joy. She was going to have to work superhard this afternoon and evening if she wanted to finish her design in time to turn it in tomorrow. But at long last she'd found a project she believed in and really *wanted* to do. She felt *mega*-inspired. Hooray!

Back in her dorm room after class, Calliope worked on drawing her museum. She kept the temple-like exterior she'd sketched when she'd first decided to design a library. However, as a tribute to her sister Muses, she now added statues of all of them across the top edge of the building's peaked roof. She hoped it wasn't showing off to include a statue of herself, but this was a MUSEum after all, and she was a Muse.

Each of the statues held a symbol of the art they represented. For example, she gave her sister Clio, the historian, a scroll; Urania, a celestial globe; and Polyhymnia, who wrote hymns, a veil. She hummed happily as she unrolled more of her planscroll and began to sketch the interiors of various rooms, labeling the collections they'd contain.

When her stomach started growling, she realized hours had passed. She'd been so absorbed in her project that she'd totally forgotten to go downstairs for dinner. Just then someone knocked on her door. "Come in!" she called from her desk. "Especially if you have food!" she joked, wondering who it could be.

The door opened, and Amphitrite poked her head in. "Actually, I do have food," she said cheerfully. She'd brought Calliope a dinner tray from the cafeteria.

"You're a mind reader!" Calliope said appreciatively as Amphitrite set the tray on her desk. It held a plate with heaping portions of nectaroni and cheese, ambrosia salad, and two pieces of delicious rosemary-olive bread.

"Didn't see you at dinner," Amphitrite said with a smile. "I figured you were probably working on your

Architecture-ology project and might need something to keep you going."

"Your timing couldn't be more perfect," said Calliope. "I'm starving!" Again she marveled at how alike her sister Terpsichore and Amphitrite were. Both were just so thoughtful!

Taking a break from her homework, Calliope motioned for Amphitrite to sit on her spare bed. As she dug into her nectaroni, she asked, "So how was your water park tour with Poseidon yesterday?"

Amphitrite grinned. "Superfun. I got to swim in every single one of the dozen water parks we visited. I wish my sisters could've come along. They would have loved it too!"

Calliope swallowed a bite of nectaroni. "How many sisters do you have?"

"Forty-nine."

"Wow," said Calliope, her eyes going round. "And I thought *I* had a lot of sisters! But I've just got eight."

Amphitrite laughed. "Believe it or not, I miss all of them. So I'm really happy I'll be going home to visit next weekend." She glanced curiously around Calliope's room. "Don't you have a roommate either?" she asked, her gaze lingering on the unused desk by the bed she was sitting on.

Calliope shook her head. "Ms. Hydra didn't give me one."

"Me neither," said Amphitrite. She sighed. "Back home under the sea my sisters and I each had our own rooms. Only, I liked that they were tiny and scrunched tight together within our cave. I can hardly work some-times without the sounds of my sisters around me."

"I know what you mean," Calliope said. "I'm the same way." A feeling of excitement was rising within

228

her. What if Amphitrite was thinking the same thing she was? But what about that sleeping fountain the mergirl had talked about building? *Well, nothing ventured, nothing gained,* Calliope thought. She smiled at Amphitrite. "I've been wondering . . ."

"I've been wondering . . . ," Amphitrite said at the exact same moment.

The two girls broke off. Then they giggled. Calliope and her sisters were always saying the same thing at the same time too. It was almost like she and Amphitrite were sisters! *Soul* sisters, anyway. Calliope set down her fork. "Sorry. You go first," she said.

"No, you go," said Amphitrite.

So Calliope popped the question. "Um . . . I was wondering if you . . . um . . . want to be my roommate?"

Amphitrite beamed at her and jumped to her feet. "Yes! I do!"

"But what about your sleeping fountain?" Calliope asked, jumping up too.

Amphitrite looked confused for a minute, then shrugged. "Oh, that. When Poseidon and I were out looking at water parks, I decided I didn't really need one. After all, I can swim in the MOA pool anytime. Or swim with my sisters undersea when I go home for visits. Sleeping in a fountain all by myself seemed even lonelier than having a room to myself in the dorm. At least when you want some company in the dorm, you can just open your door and go out into the hall."

"Yeah," Calliope agreed. "But us being room-mates will be a gazillion times better."

"You bet!" said Amphitrite.

They reached their hands high in the air and did a giddy high-five. *Whap!*

11

Collecting

"Want to see the poster I'm making?" Calliope asked a week later, glancing over her shoulder at Amphitrite. The sea nymph had moved into Calliope's room the day after Calliope had popped the roommate question. Now the girls were working at the two built-in desks on opposite sides of their room.

Just as Calliope had hoped, having a roommate had steadied her and made it easier to concentrate on important stuff. Like homework. When her roomie studied, Calliope studied too. Like now. They'd both been at their desks for an hour, quietly working.

"Sure," Amphitrite replied, crossing to Calliope's desk. Her turquoise hair fell forward as she bent to read aloud from the poster:

WANTED: Donations for the MUSEUM OF

THE GODS

Desired items:

—Monster parts (griffon talons, dragon teeth, serpent

tongues, boar tusks, etc.)

—Battle armor (shields, helmets, breastplates,

chain mail, etc.)

—Clothing (anything unusual or fantastic, or

with historical significance)

—Awards (trophies, medals, ribbons, wreaths)

Amphitrite nodded. "I like it. You should say where they're supposed to deliver donations, though," she suggested.

"Good idea," said Calliope, quickly adding that information. "Once the poster's finished, I'm going to hang it in the entry to the Academy."

Amphitrite went over and studied the pile of newly donated items on the floor at the end of Calliope's bed.

"It's so mega-cool that Mr. Libon and Principal Zeus chose your museum project."

"Isn't it?" said Calliope. "Now we'll both get to see our Architecture-ology projects built!"

It was only two days ago that Mr. Libon had announced in class that Calliope's project had been chosen. She'd also earned an A plus on it!

Above her desk she'd pinned the congratulatory

notes her sisters had sent upon hearing of her success: *"Good job, Little Sis! We're proud of you!"* said one note. Another said, *"Great news, Muse! We knew you could do it!"*

And just this morning Principal Zeus had stopped her in the hallway to congratulate her too. He'd told her that Hera was especially happy to hear about Calliope's museum, since it would "kill two birds with one stone," also helping Zeus out with his office-cleaning project.

"It's amazing how much stuff you've collected already," Amphitrite commented now. "Good thing I moved over here and left my room empty. Instant storeroom!"

"Yeah," Calliope agreed. "That was handy." Amphitrite's former room was perfect as temporary storage. However, today Principal Zeus had also given her another, bigger storage room at the back of the gym for large donations—such as an ancient chariot with a broken wheel that had once belonged to Helios. After she cataloged the items at the end of her bed, Calliope planned to take them to Amphitrite's old room. And then on the weekend she'd move everything to the storage room at the back of the gym.

Among the many items that Principal Zeus had donated so far were three scorched chair cushions, his Pegasus painting, and a model of the temple that had been built in his honor in Athens. Plus several tunics, including the gold one with the flowing cape that he'd worn when he and Hera had gotten married. He'd also promised Calliope an old jeweled throne of his. And Hera had located some tunics he had worn when he was a little godboy. Calliope had enough of his stuff for an entire Zeus wing!

Amphitrite picked up a lyre from the pile of items she was surveying and strummed it. "Who gave you this?" she asked.

"Apollo," Calliope told her. "Said it was his very first lyre."

She thought about adding a "musical instrument" category to her poster, but then decided it wasn't necessary, since she'd already collected quite a few instruments. Dionysus had donated a double-reeded aulos similar to the one Marsyas had played, Athena had donated a flute, and Poseidon, a drum set. There was also a set of musical pipes that the nymph Echo had gotten her friend Pan to donate.

Amphitrite put down the lyre and picked up a small knobby club, sending Calliope a questioning glance.

"From Heracles," Calliope informed her. "It was his club when he was five years old, before he got the big one he carries now."

"Aww. How cute!" said Amphitrite. She swung the club at a pillow on top of her bed and knocked it onto the floor. "You've got enough weapons to start your own war," she joked.

Calliope laughed. Her roommate was right. The pile contained an amazing number of weapons, including championship-winning bows and arrows from Apollo and Artemis, a spear from Ares, and tridents from both Poseidon and Amphitrite. These would all go into the weapons display room of the museum.

She left her desk and began to pick through the pile too. She showed Amphitrite a cool three-dimensional model of the Underworld that Hades had donated, and then she held up two scrolls.

Amphitrite quirked her eyebrows. "What are those? Old scrollbooks?"

"Better than that," said Calliope. "They're original manuscripts for *The Odyssey* and *The Iliad*."

"Fizzy!" Amphitrite exclaimed.

Calliope grinned. Amphitrite's way of speaking was just one of the many things Calliope liked about her roomie.

The manuscripts had been donated by Homer, of course. Though Calliope's museum mostly contained items from MOA students and teachers, she figured mortals would love seeing these manuscripts. After all, Homer's stories often featured the gods. He'd even autographed the manuscripts with this gratifying inscription:

To Calliope, my talented Muse and forever friend.

The words had gone a long way toward helping

her forgive his criticisms and the fact that he'd never returned her crush.

Crush? Calliope snapped her fingers, suddenly remembering some new donations she'd hung in the closet earlier so they wouldn't get crushed or wrinkled. "Hey! I forgot to show you the gowns Aphrodite and Hera donated for the costumes room!" she exclaimed to Amphitrite. "They came before you got back from class today."

She flung open her closet door. "Voila!" She'd shoved all of her own chitons to one end of her closet to make room for the donated gowns. There were a half dozen of them: three pink ones from Aphrodite and three others from Hera.

"Ooh! Look at this mega-gorgeous one!" Amphitrite held up a beautiful gold-colored floor-length chiton with a shimmering ten-foot-long train.

"That was Hera's wedding gown," Calliope informed her proudly. "She told me she made a deal with Zeus that if he cleaned up his office, she'd clear out closet space."

"Mortals are going to *flock* to your museum to see this," Amphitrite murmured, running a hand over the shimmery train. "Immortals, too. I can't believe Hera was willing to part with it."

Calliope nodded. "I couldn't believe it either," she said. "But she told me that a wedding chiton like hers wasn't anything you could ever wear to another event, so she figured others could have the pleasure of seeing it." She rummaged on a shelf for a few more items. "Look," she said, holding up a pair of long gold gloves and a gold tiara. "Hera donated these things from her wedding outfit as well."

While Amphitrite was admiring the gloves and

the tiara, a magical breeze whooshed in through the girls' open window and dropped off the newest *Teen Scrollazine*. It landed on the floor just beneath the window. Thump!

"I'll get it," said Calliope. After scooping up the scrollazine, she unrolled it to Pheme's gossip column. In the previous week's column Pheme had reported the missing Hero-ology game pieces. This week she announced that the pieces had been mysteriously returned, safe and sound.

Calliope smiled to herself. Only she and Homer knew the real story behind the disappearance and reappearance of the game pieces. She understood his devotion to his work and how those slumping sales might have driven him to make the bad decision he'd made. No lasting harm had been done. She didn't see any reason to get him in trouble. And she doubted either one of them would ever tell anyone else about his stealing—er, *borrowing* episode.

She rolled the scrollazine back up. Later she and Amphitrite would take turns reading aloud from it to each other, just like they both used to do at home with their sisters. Calliope stretched. "I'm ready to do something fun," she said.

"Me too," said Amphitrite as she carefully set the gloves and tiara back on the top shelf of the closet.

"Want to go for a . . . ," they both said at the same time.

They stopped and giggled. "You say it first," said Calliope.

"No, you," said Amphitrite.

Calliope thought for a moment. "Tell you what. We'll both say it at the count of three. One, two, three . . . a *nectar shake*," she said, at the same time that Amphitrite said, "A *swim*."

They giggled again. "Swim first, shake after?" Calliope asked.

"Deal," Amphitrite replied.

Calliope changed into her swimsuit and cover-up, but Amphitrite's chiton would transform to a swim top and her legs would morph into a tail as soon as she dove into MOA's pool. After grabbing towels, they headed out the door.

"Last one to the pool is a rotten egg!" said Calliope.

As they raced downstairs, Calliope's heart was lighter than it had ever been since coming to MOA. How lucky she was to have found such a *fizzy* roommate and friend! No more lonely days. They chatted all the time but knew how to be quiet together too. Perfect match!

And it was going to be fantastically fun to see her museum become a reality. How long would it take? she wondered. Even after the museum was built, she'd continue to collect donations. It would be an ongoing project, and that delighted her.

She and Amphitrite burst out the front door of Mount Olympus Academy into sunshine and blue skies. Like all the days ahead, this one looked bright and full of promise.

Don't miss the next adventure in
the Goddess Girls *series!*

Coming Soon